M000209355

ENJOY

Also by Benjamin Font

I AM NO ONE: A Collection

which includes:
THE GOOD LIFE OF A HOLY IDIOT
THE DOGS COME WHEN YOU'RE GONE
SEX/ABSURD
SONGS: I CAN'T SING
IN FULL BLOOM – *a letter, a love story*
SONS AND DAUGHTERS OF THE EARTH
I AM NO ONE – *an imaginary memoir*
TOO SOON THE SUN SETS, OLD MAN

Feature Films

SEX/ABSURD
DREAMLAND
MADNESS, FAREWELL

ENJOY
A Self-Help Book
About Anxiety

&

AT THE BOTTOM
OF THE ORCHARD
An Illustrated Fable

––––––––––

BENJAMIN FONT

The Poor House
Los Angeles

This book is a work of fiction. Names, characters, places, and incidents are the product of the author's imagination or are used fictitiously. Any resemblance to actual events, locales, persons, living or dead, is coincidental.

If you purchase this book without a cover you should be aware that this book may have been stolen property and reported as "unsold and destroyed" to the publisher. In such case neither the author nor the publisher has received any payment for this "stripped book."

First Edition of ENJOY Copyright ©2020 by Benjamin Font

All Rights Reserved. No part of this book may be reproduced in any manner whatsoever without written permission, except in the case of brief quotations embodied in critical articles or reviews.

Library of Congress Cataloging-in-Publication Data available upon request.

ISBN 978-0-578-65997-8 (pbk.)

Inquiries can be made to
THE POOR HOUSE
Los Angeles, CA
PoorHouse.The[at]gmail.com

Or under the Contact link at www.benjaminfont.com

26 25 24 23 22 21 20 19

For
A lot of people
But also, for the first time,
Myself

ENJOY
A Self-Help Book
About Anxiety

INTRODUCTION

The first time I met Eli Mallick he was holding a knife and I disliked him immediately. The two things are unrelated aside from them both being imperative details in setting the foundation of who he is and more importantly who he is to me.

The knife is important not only in that mentioning a knife so early on in a story suggests a certain amount of impending doom—physical or spiritual or otherwise—but also in that it was actually just the knife blade that he held, the handle having broken off some time ago, which he utilized very skillfully as if it were a giant razor blade to chop onions for a stew. He was a resourceful and persistent man with grit. Generous too. I liked that.

The fact that I mention disliking him then should be considered all the more important in that it stems from the same disdain that I have for mirrors—a trait he also shares. Not that I felt like I was looking at myself, but more that I was looking into a reflection, which no matter how well you think you know yourself will always seem to be distorted. Nothing ever quite lives up to its expectations.

Naturally, we became close. Suspicions were quickly confirmed that somewhere in the cosmos our souls had previously crossed paths and this new friendship was simply a manifestation of something long overlooked within ourselves. I may not have always liked him, but I loved him. Our struggle was one in the same and the time had come to tend the gardens of our dumb, sensitive hearts.

In the same way that mirrors only reflect a distorted version of ourselves, so too are others reflected in the stories we tell about them. Anxiety is a real bitch. And with nothing but love for that beautiful bitch Eli Mallick, my friend, I'd prefer to let him tell this story because it's his story and I'd like to avoid any possibility of the details being confused as my own.

This is your story, Eli. And from here I send you onward with what I believe to be the words of one of America's current sweethearts, Jennifer Lawrence:

"May the odds be ever in our favor."

Godspeed, sir.

—BF

DISCLAIMER

With the utmost respect for you, the reader, and yet a deeper bond formed between us in our shared experiences of the mental and physical anguish caused by anxiety, I, the writer, wish at once to establish our relationship as one of a straight forward and candid nature. In order to do so, I must admit that as the writer of this Self-Help Book About Anxiety, I know no one more desperate for a Self-Help Book About Anxiety than Myself, citing this unfortunate emergence from my proud retirement of "this type of writing" as the only proof needed.

That being said, if this book has found its way into your hands, then the battle I march into will have been won(the alternative I dare not mention), and there will be no one more desperate then for a Self-Help Book About Anxiety than You. It is this comforting thought that I will carry with me henceforth, like a picture of a loved one kept in the band of a helmet, or in a wallet, or on a cellphone background, because I'm really fucking scared to go into this shit alone....

—Elijah Mallick

I

THE FACT THAT YOU EXIST is pretty fucking crazy. Let's not be so casual about it. No matter what you believe about *how* you got here, it remains that you *are* here in a body whose complicated minutiae it is unnecessary to delve into, at least for now, because a mere glance in that direction could derail this whole thing completely. To concentrate too closely on the breathing, for instance...shit. It's shallow. My throat is tightening—it's going to close. What did I have for lunch? Have I developed a new allergy? My heart is beating too fast, and hard. Five...ten...fifteen. Twenty times four. That's 80 beats per minute. The common resting heart rate is between 60 and 100 beats per minute. You're fine. Relax. Just breathe. Don't think about it. Look around you:

> The bird glides into the tree.
> The tree rustles in the wind.
> The wind blows gently my hair.
> I fear that I am balding.

When did that happen? In youth, it was always wishing you were older. The capability of growing a fuller beard, of distinguished crow's feet, etc. Now it's wishing you were younger. But when did that time pass where within it you should have been of ideal age and in ideal shape? Of course, it should be now. At 28, you've made it past that wicked age where geniuses are said to die, and you've yet to cross into your thirties where it's sometimes said the loftier of dreams will die. It should be now, but it isn't. Instead, each day is an excruciating struggle to live. It is approached in the manner of a 14 year old who sneaks out of their home in the night, roaming through the dark with balled fists because danger lurks around every corner. To survive is to succeed. How abominable. The fact that you exist *is* pretty fucking crazy. But not only do you exist, if you're reading this right now then you most likely exist safer and more comfortably than 97% of the human population inhabiting this earth. That number isn't exactly known to me, nor do I care to Google it at the moment, as it seems a reasonable enough guess that the percentage is somewhere around there, and that's *really fucking crazy.*

But let's lay it all out there. *If you're reading this right now*, we can at once surmise two things: 1) You need some fucking help(who doesn't), and 2) You have the means to purchase this book, which may or may not help you, but at the very least would be a nice thing for the coffee table, the nightstand, or the bathroom. It is highly suggested that you take care of this transaction immediately(See Above: Item 1). And not just for yourself, but for those around you, your loved ones. This affliction affects 1 out of 5 Americans. The other 4 have no fucking clue how to cope with the usually invisible agony that their loved ones endure, which would make a book like this helpful to them too, and therefore 5 out of 5 Americans could use this book. That's a lot. Roughly 324 Million and growing in fact—but who's counting.

And since we're all here, how could those of you known as "the others" ever know how to cope? Those with trembling hands and short breath, ask yourselves through gritted teeth, "How could they?" If we're calling things what they are, then we're calling Anxiety a Mental Illness. Like every-thing, it occurs first in the brain before it fans out like a wildfire through the dry valley of the body's *complicated minutiae.* The twisted psyche drops the match upon itself and we're all burning from the inside out. No one can see the fire—*how could they?* There's no smoke. There's no visible panic. And if you don't know it's there, then you can't put it out.

General knowledge of fires suggests they should be smothered. There's a grease fire on the stove, so you throw a lid on that bitch. When they're small it's effective. Don't be shy. Hug me. Throw your arms around this anxious little bitch—for 20 seconds at least. Feel the oxytocin creep through the valley like a cool fog soothing everything…. You're healthier than you think. Your brain won't let your body kill itself. You're alright. Life is fucking beautiful.

But for all that, you know fires are unpredictable. Sometimes what starts small can spin quickly out of control and become bigger than you ever knew was possible.

II

BLOOD IS THE FIRST THING I SEE upon entering the Emergency Room at Cedars-Sinai. A slick, oily pool on the floor. And then the source of it: a fragile old man being helped into a wheelchair, a blood-soaked cloth pressed firmly to his face. Nothing about him registers except for his frailty and the blood. So much blood, bright and thick—it's everywhere. As two nurses wheel the man away, the wheelchair tire leaves behind a bloody tread mark on the stark white floor and two more nurses appear to clean up the mess.

Full name: Elijah Ashton Mallick. Date of Birth: December 21st, 1986. There's numbness in my left arm. And in my face. I'm having trouble breathing. Pressure in my chest. A typical warm and sunny day in Los Angeles in October and I'm shivering.

My mom is answering most of these questions for me, now on her third day in town from Phoenix visiting for her birthday. Last night we celebrated by attending my friend's solo, acoustic show in the intimate setting of a party bus. My girlfriend, Aubrey, and I drank a flask of cinnamon whiskey as my mom, never a drinker, sipped a root beer and listened contentedly. After the early show there was a late show, which was to be the last of the tour, so we decided to stick around for a few. My mom was fine, having switched to a lounging position in the driver's seat while perusing dating profiles on her phone, and Aubrey was relishing the opportunity to continue heckling our friend while he was in such a vulnerable position. It was this new crowd for the late show that didn't seem to be enjoying themselves, not even the girl that flew in from Atlanta just to see the show. They were all stiff, and shy, the close quarters of the party bus only adding to everyone's discomfort. Figuring I'd play the hero, I ran up the block to the liquor store and picked up supplies to lighten everyone's mood. It usually did the trick and this instance was no exception. I drank beer even though I quit awhile back because it makes me fat and gives me the worst kind of hangovers. Til 2am, I casually downed them along with the occasional nip from a fresh bottle, then on home to bed with a last "Happy Birthday" to my mom.

This morning I thought I'd fight my hangover by getting in the spirit of the Holidays, what with Christmas being only two months away, and decided a peppermint mocha would be the quickest, most effective way into the mindset even though I quit drinking coffee over a year ago due to a hypersensitivity to caffeine. And of course one wasn't enough, so I went for a second as well. Now, after a smoke in the park below the Hollywood sign, where any good host will take their out of town guests, we're in the fucking hospital because I had to pull over on the drive back down due to the overwhelming nature of all these symptoms at once: *numbness in my left arm, and in my face; trouble breathing, pressure in my chest.* As a moderately physically fit man under 30 it could only mean one thing: a heart attack. When my mom uttered the words I knew she was right, and jumping back in the car I struggled through every turn and every excruciating stoplight, somehow getting us to the ER at Cedars, which is a miracle because I was having a goddamn heart attack—I swear….

The EKG shows that everything's normal, which we learn quickly because at the hospital they, too, take symptoms such as mine seriously. My breathing checks out as well, lungs functioning at a perfect 100 percent. They give me a warm, weighted blanket to take care of the shivers and ask us to please wait to be seen by a doctor who will perform some secondary tests and blood work. I put on a yellow hospital mask because of the Ebola Epidemic, with two capital E's to ensure you understand the gravity of the situation and the certainty with which you will contract it. Then we go sit down.

Nothing happens quickly after that. Time simply passes from one painful moment to the next, each pretending to be the final period in the sentence upon my headstone…until together they form one massive ellipses and it's three hours later and I'm feeling a little better and everything speeds up again.

I'm laid up in a private room with a saline drip coming through my IV, still wearing my mask, paired nicely with a hospital gown, and watching the familiar, comforting face of Tom Hanks playing some sort of professor-turned-investigator on a small TV in the room's corner. Just as I'm sinking into the plot a technician comes into the room to do some chest X-Rays, then it's over and she's gone. Moments later the doctor arrives. She hears about my late night, the beer, the coffee, the cigarette— about driving in traffic. She hears about my past with anxiety, about how I'm releasing a book next month, and the direness of my financial situation. When I tell her I'm feeling OK now she's not surprised. The hospital mask had acted in place of the paper bag in the old breathe-into-a-bag-trick—it calmed me down. The warm, weighted blanket helped too. She tells me to drink less, get back off coffee, and to please, please stop smoking. And, in general, find a way to reduce the stress in my life. All of these things will help manage my anxiety, thus rendering another panic attack like this one less likely. Then she leaves me a pamphlet about panic attacks and excuses herself, and I guess I'm free to go too.

From a nearby chair my mom says my name, then snaps a picture of me when I look over, the yellow hospital mask hiding my embarrassed and utterly exhausted smile. On Thursday I'll post the picture as a "throwback." I'll caption it with the casual details of my mild heart attack(reminder, read: "Intense Panic Attack"), and half-jokingly inquire if anyone knows how the Tom Hanks movie ends. No one will respond to my inquiry. Nor will they realize that the image doesn't mark the end of anything, rather the continuation of something I've suffered from since I was a kid. But we'll get to all that in a second. For now I get dressed, spend my last $100 on the upfront hospital fee, then exit the building and wait for the rest of the bill to come in the mail.

III

"WHO THE FUCK ARE YOU, AND WHY," I whisper into the rearview mirror at my thirteen year old reflection. I'm dead serious and desperate for answers. The car is parked outside of a grocery store in Florida while my mom and grandma are inside, leaving me all alone in the car to have made this grave mistake of looking into the mirror—long and deep. My face is hot with fear. Of course I recognize the boy in the mirror as myself, but that only begs the question further: *who the fuck am I, and why?*

This is the moment I first contemplated my existence and it's terrifying. The fact that I happen to be in Florida is the icing on the cake. A horrifying moment in a horrifying place. I stare into my dark brown eyes and it only gets worse. What's behind them? And what's behind *that*? What's behind everything in general? If it all went away, where would it go? The image of a black hole comes into my mind. Within it, another black hole. And so on and so forth. Everything being sucked into an infinite vacuum. Nothingness, and nothingness, and nothingness…. An image I'll never quite shake.

With my eyes squeezed tightly shut, I hop out of the car and begin pacing aimlessly in the parking lot. I don't understand what's happening. My legs are wobbly and my mouth is dry. The black hole keeps swallowing up the idea of life itself and I can't turn it off. I can't shut it up: *who the fuck am I, and why?*

"What're you doing?" My mom and grandma are staring at me with curious smiles as they each hold a bag of groceries. I tell them nothing, just pacing around—I felt weird…. It won't be til much later that I'll realize this was my first panic attack. The only thing I knew then was that it was terrifying, and that I would avoid mirrors from then on out—I swore to it.

Typically a man of my word, the promise I made to myself about the mirrors is one that I have failed to keep on a number of occasions throughout my life. It was one such instance of failure that officially set this whole thing into motion just moments ago, only the mirror was a black one made by the flat screen TV before turning it on with plans of binge-watching The Gilmore Girls, which has been a longstanding escapism ritual of mine.

It's a month after my hospital visit and I'm still suffering from aftershocks of the big quake in my nervous system that sent me there in the first place. The bill arrived in the mail with a preposterous total of $4,657.98—two more digits than currently held in my bank account. I'm wearing heavy sweats, a sweater, and slippers. I dabbed some essential oil on the inside of one of the yellow masks that I took from the hospital and it now covers my face as if to shield me from the toxic gas that is what, *Existence*? I'm holding a glass of red wine. It's 1pm on a Tuesday. I'm about to hit the power button on the TV and slip into the safe haven known as Stars Hollow, but my gaze shifts for a moment into the dark screen and it's too late. Starting at the eyes above the mask, then all the way down to the be-slippered feet, I see it all.

This is pathetic. This isn't life. One day at a time, crawling on hands and knees like it's the 26th mile in a marathon and they stopped serving water. No shit they did, 'cause everyone else already finished six hours ago when I was waking up in awe that I'm still alive—but also scared by the fact. No one's even standing at the finish line because they've long since taken down the posts and cleaned up. Where is the finish line anyway? Now I'm pissed. Not at anyone in particular, just the blind rage of How and Why and all that shit you have the privilege of contemplating when survival is simply a given.

Fuck this. I turn on the TV, but Gilmore Girls is ruined. All I can think about is how Rory can somehow see the same thing I saw in the black mirror and how she's thinking what a pitiful monster I am. Worse, smart girl that she is, she's right. And now I'm really fucking pissed. This can't go on. I stand up and go to my typewriter, blowing off the dust and leaving the TV volume on low as I sit down and begin to write the disclaimer to what I've decided to call a Self-Help Book About Anxiety.

Carrying on though, or more precisely, returning to the topic of mirrors. I'm not the only one, nor will I be the last, to have an outright abhorrence of them. The man Borges himself once said, "mirrors and copulation are abominable, since they both multiply the number of men…."

We see eye to milky eye on the former, as I've made abundantly clear, but it's the latter where things get shaky.

If you're looking for a visual transition, imagine a man's eyes focused in the mirror in a close-up. Now picture a wider image of the same man, only you can see that he is naked and a woman rides on top of him, both watching in the mirror. I'd like to leave genders open to the reader's preference, but in this case the physical act requires one male and one female, given that we're moving on to "copulation" inasmuch as it led to your existence, which, need I remind you, is pretty fucking crazy.

Transition: one thing going into another….

Sex then. Not the very real issue of overpopulation. Just sex. Without love, or hate, or kink. *One thing going into another.* It's at the base of everything. At the tip: the individual's sexuality, and all its strange effects on the human psyche, which molds reality as a whole.

The reality of my discovery of sex is that it happened way too young. Whatever age you are in first grade—6 or 7? First by way of an old VHS, with static and hair everywhere, then by way of a friend's brother, older by 6 or 7 years, as the tape played nearby. Names and handsy details spared, whatever your reaction is to that I've experienced it as well. Shame, anger, disgust, anger, etc. For a certain period of time I dissociated from the memory altogether, which I'm certain is common practice and wildly unhealthy.

Compound that repression with the ideology of Mormonism or many other popular religions and you've got yourself a good ol' fashioned recipe for disaster. Not that I've ever considered myself a Mormon, but I was certainly baptized as one. At the wise, capable of making my own decisions age of 7—or was it 8? Whatever age you are after the first grade, which as we know is a delicate, formative age wherein the things that happen can fuck you up for life. It must have been in the water during the baptism. The terms and beliefs of the religion may not have penetrated my heart, but they definitely got under my skin—soaked right through it. If you drink and smoke, you're going to hell. God forbid you have sex before marriage....

That must've been why I waited even if I didn't realize it at the time. All through high school I had been with my girlfriend, and that was the decision we made together—to wait. Until one day she got sick, then went through chemo, and when she eventually got better shit was too serious for two kids so we broke up and I lost my virginity on my 18th birthday to a girl I'd barely known for two weeks. It was a surprise to me too. I found out when I woke up from a blackout and she was on top of me, the smell of two untouched McChickens on the nightstand next to us, which she had thoughtfully brought over when she snuck in. I put a stop to it at once with my deepest apologies. When she left, confused, I silently ate the McChickens in the dark, which had long since gone cold and thus secured my fate of feeling even shittier the following morning.

It became my thing after that, of getting drunk and committing what my subconscious believed to be a mortal sin. My resolution was absolution, by way of writing the names of the girls I'd been with on a piece of paper then burning it…and submerging myself in the warm waters of the bathtub with a little prayer: "Hail Mary, full of grace, the Lord is with thee. Blessed art thou amongst women and blessed is the fruit of thy womb, Jesus. Holy Mary, mother of God. Forgive us sinners, now and at the hour of our death. Amen."

My God! Such a dramatic little babe. But a clean one too, all fresh and new, unaware that the next mistake would be made in the next 2 to 4 weeks—always. Rinse. Repeat.

I suppose I've always been a man of habit then, even if some of them are inherently bad ones. Even the use of these Christian terms is simply out of a practiced routine, ingrained in me long before I knew what was happening. "God" itself really just means Unknowable or Unfathomable, and I do believe the Bible has my back on that. It's not a Man or a Woman, it's just a really big fucking mystery that you'll most likely spend your whole life contemplating. Unless you have what some call Faith, and in that case you're a lucky son of a bitch that better be peaceful and non-judgmental in that Faith.

It didn't dawn on me that the use of this type of language might label me in some way until I was in a small book store in Portland years ago. A little novella of mine had been placed on the shelves, and I happened to be in the store when two men bumped into each other while one was there looking for it. The other had been the head of the Big P Book Store indie section that had refused to carry this very novella. It was all such a strange coincidence. When Man No. 1 picked up the book, he asked his friend if he knew anything about it. Man No. 2 replied with perfect disdain, "I don't know. Some bullshit small Christian press thing, I think?"

My blood boiled. My face got hot. I left the store immediately and with my eyes squeezed tightly, I paced aimlessly on the sidewalk. My legs were wobbly and my mouth dry. Until I finally calmed…and stopped in front of the store window. I stared through my reflection in the glass at Man No. 2 inside, so pompous and assuming, and I whispered, "Who the fuck are you? And why?"

I was dead serious, but suddenly I didn't give a shit about an answer.

IV

THE ONLY PERSON I LIE TO IS MYSELF. I've said it a thousand times and I'll keep saying it until the words themselves become a lie because I have become truth itself and can finally shut up for good. As I told you before, I value this relationship and intend to maintain it as one of a *straight forward and candid nature*. And since we're being honest, this is the only relationship I've ever been able to hold down as such. Not for lack of trying either, or at least the desire to try.

Fuck. That reminds me. There's something I have to tell you. But where to begin…?

You'd be right to assume that we had already begun a few chapters back. The truth is, that was a long time ago and at this point it feels like beginning all over again. So much time has passed. So many people have been hurt. So many people have died. Some I've known, others I didn't and never will. Don't let this discourage you. Rather, let this be a beacon of hope. Because in all this time, I've managed to stay alive. My brain has not turned upon itself. The anxiety has yet to kill me. We have a fighting chance.

A lot has happened in the massive gap between III and IV. For starters, The Book came out. I DON'T EXIST. Perhaps you've read it, but probably not. It was accompanied by a campaign of short videos entitled "Dear Famous People," in which I made absurd pleas to celebrities to endorse the book in hopes that their names alone would fool people into clicking Play, which would obviously result in them purchasing my book. It didn't work.

Next, my first "real" movie got made. One I wrote for a buddy awhile back under the title "Mother Fucker." He wound up directing it, they finished the movie, and eventually it enjoyed a limited theatrical release before finally settling into the Streaming World, where it is currently available. Maybe you've seen it, and if you haven't you should—right after you finish this book.

Then there was my movie, which I wrote, directed, and starred in. A little feature with the cute, ironically high-brow title of FOLIE, ADIEU. A pun indeed, layering in French nonetheless, playing off the term *folie a deux*, which means "shared madness" or "madness of two," while the direct translation is actually a wave goodbye to that madness. A farewell, if you will. In short, it's about two characters who are determined to off themselves during the holidays. A light affair. We shot it in just eight days on location here in LA last December for under $40k, turned the edit around quickly, and are currently in the final stages of post-production hell. It's now late June. Nothing can be done until the movie is completed.

One year after my trip to the hospital I was finally able to pay off the bill thanks to Cedars being understanding to my financial situation by dramatically decreasing the amount I was to pay, as well as an installment agreement that was very similar to the one I still have with the IRS for tax years starting three years ago. I followed the doctor's orders to a T, in that I mean I came to the T and couldn't make a decision of which way to turn so just kicked it into reverse and hit the gas. Still drinking. Still smoking. Not drinking coffee, but also not doing a very good job of relieving the self-imposed stressors of work as evidenced in the above three paragraphs which focused solely on work. Some things never change. Age is not one of them. I successfully entered my thirties *where it's sometimes said the loftier of dreams will die*—etc. etc.

Moving forward, it is my duty to acknowledge that my uncanny ability to skirt the issue is another one of those things that has not changed—at all. But I am determined to change that now because the only thing scarier than change is to be stuck, and if I get stuck here then I'm really fucked. Here in my studio in Koreatown, alone, smoking indoors and drinking rosé like it's the fucking 1940's.

When I moved to Los Angeles I lived on the concrete floor of a loft downtown that six or seven other people inhabited. I was never alone. Shortly thereafter, I met Aubrey and we quickly celebrated that day(and into the following morning) as our anniversary. First one month, then two, three, four, five, and six months. Then a year. Then two, three, four, five, and six years. We lived together. We were never alone. We had each other and our two dogs. But the foundation was cracked.

I remember drinking together in her kitchen not long after we first met and I told her that I wasn't ready for the next big thing. I was still hung up on my ex and an absolute mess, with the added bonus that *I lived on the concrete floor of a loft downtown that six or seven other people inhabited.* Not to mention I didn't have a phone, or a computer, or a job. Though I didn't say any of that aloud other than that *I wasn't ready for the next big thing.* Unfortunately, to this day I'm positive that she must have only heard The Next Big Thing. And she was it.

It's strange to think about how easy it is to fuck each other up. It's as simple as breathing. If we don't think about it, it's bound to happen. And even worse when you *do* think about it—it's short and uneven. And then long and withheld for too long…. Just let it out…and then in. Out…and then in….

The fountain pisses on itself in the courtyard.

The courtyard welcomes all of the visitors.

The visitors laugh like everything's OK.

None of them are here to see me.

Now I'm always alone. Which is a problem, because I've never learned how to be like this—alone. It's always been one relationship to the next, then on to another, with a long cross dissolve between that leaves everyone heartbroken and time is questionable at best. So much time has passed. And at this point, *it's like beginning all over again.*

At the start we were invincible. Probably because we had set the precedent of calculated miscommunication, allowing ourselves to only hear what we wanted to hear and in so becoming only what the other wanted us to be. What a charming story(that I don't want to hear about), how you disappeared to small town Texas for two weeks where you met a married girl named Maria, who you became entangled with, then went to Austin where her ex-boyfriend tattooed your last name on her ribs. And how sweet that you appeased her by getting that tattoo of her name on your chest, only adding an "Ave" before the "Maria."

Ave Maria, that familiar sinner's prayer: "Hail Mary, full of grace, the Lord is with thee. Blessed art thou amongst women and blessed is the fruit of thy womb, Jesus. Holy Mary, mother of God. Forgive us sinners, now and at the hour of our death. Amen."

WE should get tattoos. So we did, Aubrey and I. Her with the cursive "M" from Mallick in my signature on the side of her finger, and me with her last name on my inner bicep next to the place where St. Francis has stood since I was twenty-one: "Cuore." Funny thing about that is, St. Francis has a very famous prayer himself that begins,

"Most high, glorious God, enlighten the darkness of my **heart**...."

Or in his native tongue, Italian: "Dio più alto, glorioso, illumine l'oscurità del bio **cuore**...."

Cuore, indeed. The ever persistent need to make sure the back door is unlocked in case of emergency when entering through the front. A quick trip to a local parlor and the lovers' tattoo could be undone, morphed into St. Francis' prayer that concludes: "...and give me true faith, certain hope, and perfect charity, sense and knowledge, Lord, that I may carry out Your holy and true command."

What is truth? Whose commands do we follow anyway? We think that we're free, but really we're all victims of our own impulses. We didn't get enough attention as kids or our parents were never proud enough so we're always seeking that validation through someone else. It won't come, at least not to the extent that it's needed. Even if it does come, deep down we feel like we don't deserve it. Not here. Not now. So we plan our exit strategy in the back of our minds, and before we even know it we're hopping the fence in the backyard and rushing to the neighbor's house....

A single light is on. The husband isn't home. Suddenly a phone rings. It's my dad on the line: "Do you blame me for fucking your shit up?"

"What?"

"Do you blame me for fucking you up."

"Uh...no. But if I went to a therapist I might."

He laughs. It's my laugh. He gave it to me. And I laugh too in the same way, but as we're on the phone I'm realizing this isn't the only thing he gave me, his physical attributes aside. He gave me some of his shit—as we all do. He passed down the heaviness of his own upbringing and I went mad with the same uncertainties he must have suffered himself, only in his case with added trauma that's not my place to mention. And I don't blame him. We're all creatures of habit, built to repeat the mistakes of others because at least we understand what to expect from those mistakes.

I'm sorry I quit baseball. I'm sorry I took for granted everything you provided. I'm sorry you're not proud of me. Or maybe you are, but I'm sorry it didn't feel that way in the past. I do know you love me, even if historically it's been the tough kind.

"Jesus, dude. You might."

But I wouldn't. I might blame his parents though. They were terrible. Fuck them. And fuck their parents. Fuck everybody. Also, fuck me. *Especially* fuck me. My shit is mine alone to take responsibility for. I have hurt, because I am broken. I'm sorry. I'm so fucking sorry. And I'm broken because I've never taken the time to fix it. When do you do that anyway? And how?

Presumably alone, for starters. *But I never learned how to be alone.* Even now, I am not alone. It is you who keeps me company in this darkness, sitting on my sofa while *smoking indoors and drinking rosé like it's the fucking 1940's.* A captivated audience in my imagination, commiserating with me through the night in the hope that morning will bring happiness, contentment. It doesn't matter if you're real or not. As they say, the imagination is a powerful thing. When it comes to ourselves, we are all exceptional liars.

V

I IMAGINED A DIFFERENT FUTURE and because it doesn't align with the reality of the present I must endure this perpetual discontent. I'm not happy and never fully satisfied. I'm lucky as hell, but still haven't won the lottery. And I could really use the money.

It's the 1st of July and rent is due. A modest $1,400 for my very well kept and decorated 350 square feet. That's $4 per square foot if you want to break it down, or about 3-cents per square inch if you really want to have fun. The current balance in my checking account is $1,388.33, which works out to afford roughly 347 square feet of my studio. That leaves the other 420 square inches of the place up in the air, which I'd say is a sign to relax and all will be fine, but I can't smoke pot because it just exacerbates my anxiety. Looks like the bathroom sink will have to go then. Or better yet, the tiny kitchen stove. I've stopped cooking these days anyways.

As the one year anniversary of discovering this little gem approaches, it's impossible to not reflect on not only the events of the past 12 months, but also the events which led to the necessity of finding this apartment in the first place. For the sake of brevity, and also a bit out of fear, I won't go back too far—less than a decade, for sure. Still, what I'm about to tell you will decidedly make me look bad. Certainly you've had your heart broken…but have you ever broke it yourself?

As I mentioned previously, when I met Aubrey I was a complete mess. "It" had become my thing again: *of getting drunk and committing what my subconscious be-*

lieved to be a mortal sin. And habits are hard to break. Plus, there was nothing about the circumstances of our meeting that should've indicated it was to be taken seriously. At some shitty Hollywood club though neither of us identify with that type of scene? It was a rare occurrence, but there we were at the same place and at the same time and both very drunk off the same bottle that belonged to a very distant but mutual acquaintance. Her first words to me were, "You're the best looking guy here and I want to kiss you."

"Then do." And she did. All the way into the bathroom, then out into my friend's car as he was driving us back to her place. We accidentally kicked over her bong in the bedroom when we got there. The water went everywhere. But we didn't care and continued because the future could be as bright as our imaginations. By morning we both woke up with huge question marks over our heads, which were answered shortly when we turned over and saw each other with relief. Then we brushed our teeth together, she slipped a little bracelet onto my wrist, and put cash in my pocket for cab fare.

We walked her dog together before I took off. She got coffee while I waited outside the grocery store with the pup. Then she went to work and I left in a cab…hopping out long before making it back to the loft downtown *where I lived on the concrete floor of a place that six or seven other people inhabited.* Why wouldn't I? That meant I saved some cash and was able to call a buddy from a payphone(sic) and offer him a pack of smokes for the ride while still pocketing $20 for myself. Jesus, what an asshole. In any case—

What was an emotional little wreck like me to think while on that ride back to the loft? Had I just met the one? Or was this just a one night stand that would bleed into the next day or the next week or month, who knows—*time was questionable at best*. And still is. I can say that with certainty because only a moment ago when I was writing this it was the 1st of July and now here we are on the 13th—what the fuck....

The interim can only be described in the fashion of a parking lot. Noting spots J1, J2, then J3, and so on to J12 as if they were a make, model, and year that must be catalogued in order to keep track of the keys. Never lose the keys. And all this metaphorically of course, because I never drive after a drink and I've definitely had way too many.

J1 might be considered a 2014 Mercedes Sprinter van, as it began while I was at work at the antique furniture Galerie on a Saturday. Afterwards the thing was parked and I found myself heading to a nearby tequila and taco joint with Cain, a buddy of mine from the Galerie. But we weren't alone. *I never learned how to be alone.* There was a girl with us, and her sister. The girl's name was Lara. We met only a few weeks ago at a book release party at the Galerie where her skin was pale and her lips were red and the drinks were good and free. She repeated my lines with her own inflections naturally as if we'd known each other forever. What a fine misconception to allow yourself. We knew nothing about the other. The perfect time to pretend. Really just...patterns.

Next thing I know it's J2 and we're waking up together. The previous night had led me, Cain, and Lara to a tattoo parlor downtown where her friend, Eva, was getting her first tattoo. As well as her second and third. Lara's sister had chosen wisely not to join. So now it's J2: a 2017 Toyota Prius with all leather interior and a cooler in the trunk stocked with enough cold beer and rosé for all four of us to get drunk.

From there it becomes a fucking mess if you hadn't guessed. Or had it begun that way regardless? With J3 being an Audi rental because the BMW got rear-ended and J4 being an open parking space because the car is lost altogether.

J4: Independence Day. Last year I spent it alone on a friend's couch where I was crashing while they were out of town. Everything had just exploded at home and I found myself scrambling for a new place to live after five years of living together with Aubrey. The fireworks were amazing that night. Or so it seemed from the noises outside, as all I could see inside was the glow from the TV, and even that was bleary with booze and tears. The neighbors were throwing a party. I could hear the girls laughing and wished badly that I would be invited. Now one year later and we celebrate this Independence as a broken foursome, with all of us having latched onto one another as a co-dependent group as if there might be some healing found in the others' wounds. We're all going through a break up, or a divorce. We're all fucked up. It's a beautiful nightmare.

But this is all just a distraction, a quick detour through the confusing dark country of broken hearts. It's unsustainable. The tank is draining fast. We're bound to run out of gas. And what then? When we find ourselves out in the middle of nowhere and finally realize that we've gone too far to turn back. We forced our hands and exhausted all our options. The homes we built no longer exist, but only because we abandoned them and they went to shit. Not because we wanted to either. But because we couldn't bear knowing that we didn't deserve it.

Was she the one? How could I have waited to ask that question? Even though I cheated, I couldn't find the answer. And really...This Is Not A Test.

As I said, when I met Aubrey I was a complete mess. Old habits were hard to break. It took three months before I even considered that was an option. We were back in her kitchen again, drinking as we once had been. *I wasn't ready for the next big thing*—Her. But I had already fucked it up so much. How could you build on that foundation? Only she didn't see the cracks, so I vowed silently to myself that I would change. I patched up what I could and we moved forward with construction.

I got better then. For awhile at least, as long as I could hold out. But the demons were so deeply rooted like weeds that they survived the surface cleaning. Every six months or so they would grow back. No matter how much I loved her, I couldn't kill them. Some small thing would happen and "It" was triggered again. I'd get drunk and manage to self-destruct. Only she never knew, and when my head cleared I promised myself this time would be different.

Six years passed that way, for better or worse, and still we were together. She and I and our two dogs, the second one having been adopted together. It was good, which perhaps was part of the problem. I loved her too much to leave and lied to myself too much to realize I wasn't changing. I should probably go to therapy. But there's the matter of money and not having insurance, and I actually can't think about all that right now, my God….

Sweat beads gently down the glass.

The glass is taken up into my hand.

My hand trembles violently.

I'm always afraid that I'll spill.

My subconscious is a real motherfucker. I should've seen what it was cooking. It didn't smell good, but there was still no way of getting out of it. I was going to have to eat the whole goddamn thing.

I'm addicted to distractions. They provide just enough amusement to avoid confronting the real issues at hand. But when this one came, I could sense that something was different. If you listened carefully, you could even hear the patches ripping apart at the seams beneath the basement floor. Her name doesn't matter. Maybe none of this matters. But if I want to be able to breathe then I have to get this giant fucking elephant off my chest.

It started with a "Poke" on a certain social media app. I reciprocated and suddenly she messaged. We had met briefly years ago when I first moved to LA. We had mutual friends. It was all just an innocent check in. Until a month later when she suggested we meet. I felt that I was spiraling in her illusion and could only squash that illusion by facing her in reality—so we met. Casually, just for a smoke in the middle of the day. Ten minutes. My heart sunk and my mind raced: *What the fuck are you doing? This isn't what you want. This isn't good. Just fucking stop.*

After we hugged goodbye I sighed with relief. It was over. I would never have to see or talk to her again and life could go back to normal because I finally faced it and didn't like what I saw. I loved my life. I loved Aubrey. I loved our two sweet little dogs. There was nothing in this world worth jeopardizing that. Unfortunately, that too didn't matter. Because when she texted one night a week later and Aubrey was asleep next to me as usual, I decided—drunk and lonely—to take her up on the offer and left a cheap, poorly worded note for Aubrey on the bedside table before leaving.

The following morning I crawled back into bed next to Aubrey at 6.30am and fell asleep. At 7am she woke me up with my phone in her hand, tears streaming down her face. She didn't yell. I wish she had. Instead she read a series of messages that had been exchanged by me and this girl, concluding with "And it just keeps going and going, what the fuck?" What the fuck is right. The dinner bell was ringing and my subconscious had served its shit up piping hot. Time to eat.

My mom happened to be passing through town that morning, in the middle of her own nightmare of a move from Arizona up to Washington accompanied by her very own piece of shit boyfriend that clearly *didn't* love her. I guess we all have our types…our patterns…. My tearful conversation with Aubrey was interrupted by my obligation to go meet them for breakfast. I could hardly eat with my stomach like that. My mom was under the impression my mood was because of her boyfriend, and there was no way I could tell her the truth about my situation. About the situation I had caused.

When they took off she left me with two boxes of things from her house that she sold in Arizona: one was full of old pictures from my childhood, and the other was filled with an extensive set of China that had been from her wedding with my dad. Which in hindsight, though still terrifically sad, turned out to be a blessing because as of that day I would need to find a new place to live and furnish it with my own things. Dishes had just been checked off the list. Just one less thing to worry about, I suppose....

I told Aubrey I was leaving when I got back to our place with the boxes from my mom. It was the only thing to do in that moment. Not that it was For anyone, or that it was a good thing at all, it was truly just *the only thing to do in that moment*. I hated saying it, and I hated doing it even more. But I did it: through tears I threw my shit into a duffel bag and took off. It was so hot that day. The sun was so bright.

A week or so later at our apartment, I told Aubrey everything. Each and every little fuck up that had been buried throughout the course of our relationship. She saw just how broken I was and it was the closest we had ever been. I had never loved her more than that day. She had never really seen me before. She didn't want to at the start, so I hid myself accordingly...but she saw me then. And I saw her for how understanding and truly loving she could be. She saw me, and still didn't want me to go. But staying wasn't an option. Not a viable one at least, one that might lead to anything positive in the future. I had to go. My new apartment was waiting, and the space felt necessary for us to mourn each other and decide what to do with that mourning.

This isn't the future I had imagined, but I'm aware that my inclinations are highly susceptible to a romanticized version of any given future and it is very possible that I will always suffer from this disappointment of expectations unmet. Who knows.

Or as my brother Marlon says, "While the scientific habit of mind is one of disciplined imagination, the artistic one is imagination unfettered. What the artistic imagination lacks in its approximation of the real world it makes up for in its complete freedom to go anywhere. Orgasms and hell—etc." Here we are.

If you want to go, I don't blame you. I'd leave myself if I could. Still, I beg of you: please stay….

VI

THIS IS ALL JUST ONE BIG OCEAN. What's the difference if you're six feet under the surface or six inches? You're still under water. If you haven't drowned yet you just have to keep kicking. The only option is to fight.

The water is warm from the sunlight. I'm close to the top, but my arms are tired. My legs are cramped from the continuous struggle. Darkness clouds my periphery as my consciousness begins to waver. If only there were a hand to help pull me up the rest of the way. I can see it there, rippling just above the surface. One finger dips under to just the first knuckle. It caresses my forehead with the weight of a ton of bricks. Promising and damning all at once.

That is the seduction of this city. The uncanny ability to stay at a very close, yet impossible distance like an apparition in a dream. This is definitely a dream. But no one ever tells you it's actually going to be a nightmare. One that entraps you with both real and false hope, almost identical in nature to the point that you're scared to call it by name because you're not sure which twin you're talking to. Is it Mary Kate or Ashley?

"Hi, I'm Ashley." She says it sweetly and extends a tiny hand as I introduce myself as well. Then she goes into the other room.

"That answers that question," I think to myself as I stand there alone in her living room. It's so peaceful. Out the wall of windows there is nothing but green, thriving plant life and vegetation as though the drought had never existed here. Amongst the green is a beam of sunlight where within it two white butterflies flutter in gentle chaotic unison. As I watch them, my thoughts fall away from me like a series of black satin sheets that finally reveal a single canvas on which a masterpiece is painted—this *one* thought: "I'm home…."

Then she comes back into the room and I remember that Brian is there with me, my friend and co-worker at the Galerie, and the only reason we're here is to deliver furniture. She politely tells us what she wants and which pieces go where, we follow her instructions, we all smile, then she tips us generously and Brian and I leave. Another day another dollar, as they say. But in this case it's $1,000 because it settles a bet from my childhood.

I had a crush on both of the twins when I was a kid. I was enamored by the idea of California and by their beauty and what they represented. My tiny heart swelled against the wide open prairie of my youth with the hope that someday I might obtain that life for myself. An innocent childhood celebrity crush that my dad quelled by insisting that I would never meet them. Mom wasn't happy about the discouragement, so pops Mallick went further by saying, "Alright—if you meet them I'll give you $1,000." And you better believe he's a man of his word. No picture necessary.

It's strange what this city does to the notion of celebrity. In some ways it glorifies or exploits it, while in others it simply normalizes it—or humanizes it rather. It's both disgusting and fascinating.

I'm in no way star-struck, though certain people do elicit some feelings of great admiration for their careers and legitimate artistic accomplishments. However, when I first started at Galerie I wasn't prepared for one encounter in particular that affected me all too personally. It was during a delivery to an actor's home. But not just any actor, it was to "Mr. O— Bloom."

When I learned where we were going my palms began to sweat. Not out of some weird infatuation, but because it is with those words a certain novella of mine begins, which is a book about mistaken identity wherein the lead character allows a young woman to believe that he actually is the unnamed though obvious actor. It was this book that landed me in LA in the first place after taking it on a reading and drinking tour down the west coast from Portland. My reading in LA and the people I met there were what led to anything that followed. The book held particular importance to me in the body of my work and in my life.

"Do I give him the book?" I asked my boss, who is a very generous and kind man with an unbelievably dry sense of humor. "When would even be a good time?"

"If you're rolling around naked on the rug at the end then that would probably be when to do it," he said absurdly, then countered with a very genuine compliment to the actor's sense of humor and kind heart.

Fuck it. I printed off a copy right there at the Galerie, then loaded the table into the van and began the drive. When I got there the interior designer was moving some pieces around on the back patio with two other guys as the actor looked on and helped however he could. I didn't say a word, just unloaded the table and set to work with the designer to move some other stuff around the house. Two hours later the work was done and we were all set to leave. We said our goodbyes in the kitchen. As the others shuffled out, I was emboldened to linger a moment longer by the fact that the actor truly did have a good sense of humor and kind heart. My tongue felt heavy and there was a quiver in my voice: "Excuse me, O—" I said, calling him by his first name in his own kitchen and probably sending a shiver up his spine.

"Yeah?" He kept a smile on his face, but surely it was forced. "I wrote this book called—"

"You're a writer? Me too!" His dad said while standing to shake my hand vigorously.

"Yeah," I said, as behind Mr. Bloom the interior designer who hired me stood with a mortified, wide eyed look and a chopping hand gesture at his throat to tell me to shut the fuck up. But I had already gone too far. "And the basic idea of the book revolves around the fact that I've always been told that I look like you."

"Really…." He clearly disagreed with the statement as the interior designer shook his head in utter frustration and exited.

"Yeah, and so there's this whole confusion with identity and the guy winds up letting this girl believe that he actually is you. Anyway—I'd love to give you a copy."

"Sounds great. I'd love to give it a read."

"Perfect. I've got one in the van if I can give it to you."

"Oh." Goddamnit. Creepy. "Yeah, OK."

"Alright, I'll be right back."

When I went to retrieve the freshly printed copy of the book the designer was waiting at the van in angry disappointment. "You can't do that. These are clients. This isn't why you're here."

Those words struck a chord within me. *This isn't why you're here.* Actually, this is *exactly* why I'm here. I'm nothing if I don't utilize these opportunities, at best—by a long shot—to further my career, but at the very least to have some self-respect and not walk away with the shameful and gnawing feeling of *what if*. The circumstances were far too specific to pass up. My body suddenly stopped trembling. "But can I give him the copy? It's right here...."

He sighed. "I guess? Fine. If he said you could. Just...you can't do this again. This is my work and it reflects negatively on me."

"I understand." And I did. For fuck's sake, the whole thing was wildly inappropriate. I could've been fired and even slapped with a restraining order just out of precautionary measures. But neither was the case thankfully. The designer just walked off without another word and blacklisted me from his projects for the next six months. Fair enough. Because I would have been filled with regret had I not taken the copy back up to Bloom's door and knocked. Then waited…then knocked again. He finally answered.

"Here you go. And please, know that it's supposed to be a funny book, so…take it with a grain of salt." Yes, I said those words.

"Right then. Well, thank you." He took the book with a nod and a smile, closed the door, and probably never even read the opening line. It's doesn't matter though. It made it into his hands. He knows it exists.

All that to further illustrate the bizarre incongruity of this city, this existence. The proximity with which you are to success within your industry while being seen expressly as the help. Humbling and invigorating, it keeps you kicking even when *your legs are cramped from the continuous struggle*. It keeps you striving to rise above the surface where the air might not be clean, but at least it's fucking breathable. At least you're alive. You exist. Which, need I remind you again…*is really fucking crazy*.

Still, it's no wonder that my anxiety would've flared up again within this world. My hypersensitive heart is tugged every which way at all times. I experience not only the pain of a double life, but the confusion of multiple lives. Dichotomy is one, or really two, things—separately; polychotomy is a different beast altogether. To be a boyfriend, to be a lover, to be a friend, to be a glorified laborer, to be nothing and everything, to be a writer lost in a story he's created. This is a fiction. I am not real. Don't look in the mirror. How does one manage this? *Do Not Look In The Mirror.*

The eyes are the window to the soul.

The soul is heavy…but light.

The light is dimmed for affect.

Sometimes I fucking hate myself.

But only because I love myself so deeply that this cycle of troubling behavior is the biggest disappointment of all. Tough love has become mandatory for survival, and for change. You're not dying, you motherfucker. You're not going through this again. Give yourself 10 minutes. Live in it. Then move on. Remember, you're strong.

Oh my—my most sincere of apologies for that sudden outburst. I had gotten up to take a piss and it happened—I looked. Not on purpose of course, but it seems the mirror is sometimes unavoidable. Perhaps it's for the best to sometimes take a long and hard look. In any case, where were we?

That's right. In the ocean. How the fuck did we get here? Regardless, let's take a moment to float. Preserve energy and enjoy the strange echoes of this alien world. Take it all in now because there's no saying when it'll all be gone. And besides, to quote my brother Marlon again: "Thought cancers, tumorigenesis of the imagination, can be successfully overcome." Which sounds optimistic as fuck.

VII

WHY ARE YOU DELETING YOUR ACCOUNT? Is it because you met someone, you're not getting enough matches, you want a fresh start, something is broken? That's the obvious box to check. Yes, something is broken. Me. I am broken. Jesus. There, I said it again. Are you happy now? OK—Account Deleted.

It's 8.15am and I can barely open one eye as I delete my *Kindling* account for the fifth or sixth time this week, having reactivated it again last night in a drunken fit of loneliness just after midnight when I had finished with my work for the evening. A terrifying moment—always. The second you switch off and the brain becomes aware of its surroundings: a dimly lit studio that embodies the word Solitude. There's a fresh bottle of wine in the fridge. You nursed the first one over four hours of writing. But this one you're going to hit hard, and fast, because you're alone and never learned how to be without at least the company of your work. This has become a distraction too. Cathartic and productive, yet still just another device to deflect the real problem, which undoubtedly has quite a lot to do with why you continuously reactivate your *Kindling* account in the first place. But it's OK—*Account Deleted*.

Now a text from Aubrey. Fuck. I'm too late. It's a screen grab of my *Kindling* profile one of her friends must have sent her from the night before. Apparently *Kindling* automatically selects a few additional photos from your other social media accounts to accompany your main profile picture. It's all a new and very dangerous novelty to me. This photo in particular happens to be of us. In fact, she took it. She's lying on the floor in a hotel room in Vegas, her phone pointed up at the mirrored ceiling in order to take the picture. I'm sitting on the sofa nearby. She's written a single word beneath the screen grab: "Nice."

I suppose it was just a matter of time, and it being a year since I moved out should suggest that time has been ample and my presence on *Kindling* is totally appropriate. But, to repeat myself yet again, *Time is questionable at best*. And Aubrey follows up with another text: Already on *Kindling* just three weeks out."

Three weeks. Has it only been that long? This probably deserves an explanation, which I'll get to in a moment. I just need a second to wrap my head around this. A breath. Space. A cigarette….

I take my smoke into the grass.

The grass is littered with dog shit.

The shit reeks of neglect.

We are all guilty from time to time.

After I moved into this place a year ago, when Aubrey and I hugged goodbye she whispered into my ear, "So what do we do now? Pretend we're strangers?"

"We're meeting for the first time. We both just got out of a six year relationship. It's a fucking mess." Then I kissed her on the cheek and left.

But the departure, though significant, was explicitly physical. Emotionally, everything stuck around. *We were strangers, meeting for the first time*. Of course we got back together. The romance was a whirlwind. The trouble was that I looked a lot like her ex. Smelled a lot like him. Felt a lot like him. Acted a lot like him. Hell, I *was* him—so how could she ever trust me?

The new honeymoon lasted for five months. It was December and we hadn't seen much of each other in the previous few weeks because I had been prepping and then shooting my movie. It was the night we wrapped, 2am. I opened my eyes, heavy as hell as if the weight lifted from my shoulders had gone straight into my lids in sheer exhaustion. The sound that woke me was a FaceTime from Aubrey, in tears: "Babe, we're done. You know it."

"What?"

She just kept repeating it: "We're done. We're done."

Then again when I got to her place at 3am. *We're done*. Only she added as evidence that we hadn't seen each other in weeks and I was the happiest I'd ever been. The whole thing caught me off guard. It was late and we'd both been drinking. I was exhausted. We had just wrapped the movie, which *we shot in just eight days*. Of course I was the happiest I'd ever been. I was doing the exact thing I wanted to be doing and had worked so hard towards over the last ten years, and I was with a girl I loved more than anything in a relationship that finally felt genuine, wholesome, and transparent. However, she admitted that certain aspects of this *transparency* had been forced. My social media accounts were being monitored. Each like or comment was an obvious hint at ongoing infidelity. The password on my phone had been discovered, and each text or email suggested something more devious beneath its innocent surface.

She didn't want to live like that, and I shouldn't have to live like that either. We deserved to be happy. What was left was miserable and we couldn't continue. *We're done*. She repeated it one last time in the morning when I left, and I fucking believed it.

So why then did we spend Christmas together at her aunt and uncle's place? Why then when she left on her tropical New Year's vacation did I housesit for her and spend time with our dogs while receiving daily

FaceTimes that casually asked me if I would be out looking for a new girlfriend that night? Because I could, I was single. Why? What the fuck was happening? The truth is that I didn't know. Though if I had to take a guess now I'd say that I loved her, but I was disoriented, mad at sea, fucking lost, etc. I had finally found myself standing on my own two feet in my place in Koreatown, pursuing what I always had in my career while finally feeling some of the freedom that comes with accomplishment—however small the budget—and finally found myself in a relationship that was not only good, but sustainable…even if it was with my ex. All that and the rug was ripped out from under me. Not that it shouldn't have been a thousand times before, but it had remained there for so long it felt like it simply belonged. Only now it would be better taken care of, vacuumed daily, washed on a regular basis and such. It would last forever.

But it wouldn't. Just another six months because *the rug was ripped out from under me.* Balled up in the corner of the room it had lived in for so long, and there I found myself pissed, manifesting it through the physical act of actually pissing on the metaphorical rug. Not out of spite or malice. They were more like little accidents just like our dog would have when we were gone for too long. I would explore other options in search of a new beginning. Each would lead me back to her, where she would then pull away and I would think it was hopeless. This could never work. So I explored even more options, each with the same result that led me back to Her. Where she would set a terrifying ultimatum then pull away because it was broken. *This could never work.* It was sad, disgusting, and reckless as hell.

The best quote I have ever come across concerning this type of self-destructive behavior is one I have quoted before, but if I've taken the liberty of quoting myself repeatedly there's certainly no harm in again quoting D.H. Lawrence, who said: "Recklessness is almost a man's revenge on his woman. He feels he is not valued so he will risk destroying himself to deprive her altogether."

It doesn't matter if she actually did value me. Her reality is unfortunately of no consequence to my perception of reality because we're all stuck in our own heads and pain is subjective no matter how fortunate we are or at least appear to be to someone else. All that matters is that this experience is ours alone to live out and that what we do with our interpretations of this experience be just, peaceable, and lead to the betterment of humanity as a whole. God, I have failed….

I'm only human is no longer excuse enough. As flawed as we are, being human is also synonymous with consciousness. The awareness to make our own decisions and to change. I have made so many bad decisions. It is time to change. And failure isn't an option.

A jog to kick things off. It's been at least six weeks since my last jog on which I came across a dead cat on the sidewalk. The body was covered in so many flies that it actually appeared to move as if it were holding on to its last bit of life in hopes of a miracle. The birds knew better though. They circled overhead in a dark cloud and the whole thing all seemed laughably obvious. A set piece constructed specifically for me to stumble across. I considered taking a picture—though I can't say why that sick impulse presented itself—but decided better of it and even without the physical picture of it there's still a very real and vivid one that exists in my head.

No more of this shit though. A different day. A different jog. The same route along 6th Street between Wilton and Highland that feels like you're in a different city completely.

I'm in Portland then. I'm taking in the sunlight through the trees as my legs carry me mechanically forward. One of the trees has low, drooping branches that are supported by three metal beams like some sort of botanical cane or walker minus the tennis balls. Even the trees get old and need help sometimes. It's all life, isn't it. And death. And hilarity and depression—Hallelujah!

As I'm wondering which turn I might take to peel off and head towards the river that cuts Portland in two, my mind wanders back to all that shit about reality and how *all that matters is that this experience is ours alone to live out and that what we do with our interpretations of this experience be just, peaceable, and lead to the betterment of humanity as a whole.* How good my intentions have been. How gentle and pure my thoughts. Making the gross inconsistencies of my actions all the more disgusting—repulsive even.

I don't think I've ever hurt anyone I didn't love. And no one physically outside of an athletic setting where certain cuts and bruises are to be expected. Then again, emotional pain is certain to come with its own physical side effects. In that way, I suppose this is just another round about lie to myself. Some diversion of rhetoric or a mindless fuck to avoid addressing the plain and simple facts. Here they are:

The final break happened on a Monday morning, but began on the Saturday night prior. My hometown friend was in town with his band and they had a show at the Bootleg. It was mandatory that I attend not only out of a sense of responsibility to an old friend, but also out of a love for seeing my friends be good at what they do. Also, I had used quite a bit of his music in my movie and it would simply be in poor taste to not show my support. I convinced Aubrey to attend with me and a few of our friends joined as well because they knew the kid opening the show. Everyone had drinks in the green room beforehand and the drinks continued while the show went on. After it ended I was fairly drunk as dinner had been skipped, but I tried to maintain as we chatted with my friend and his bandmate in the crowd. Turns out they had plans of sleeping in their van that night, which disturbed me deeply that I had not stepped up to the table earlier to offer them my place in Koreatown. I had planned on staying with Aubrey anyway, so my place was empty. We agreed to hang out afterwards and they could sleep comfortably in a real bed.

Aubrey must have seen something I didn't. Something that must have been visible in my eyes after a certain number of drinks. A look that expressed I was in for the long haul even if I didn't know it yet. I went to grab another round of drinks, but when I turned back into the crowd she was gone.

I texted her: "Did you leave?"

She responded: "Yeah, I'm in a car on the way home. Stay with your friends."

This had been an issue before, but one that I thought was behind us. It wasn't often that we went out, but it had always been important for me to show support for my friends and for her to show support for me when they were performing or when the event was about me directly. No matter, she always wound up leaving early. Typically there was some sort of goodbye in prelude. Not this time, which left me confused and hurt and more than half drunk while holding two fresh drinks in hand. I finished one, then the other…and vaguely remember a text to someone in the bathroom.

Next thing I know I'm waking up in Glassell Park on a deflated air mattress in someone's living room and Lara, the girl from the Galerie party awhile back with the pale skin and red lips, is coming out of the bedroom to say good morning. It was clear nothing had happened, but that was completely beside the point. She offered me water, but what we both really needed was a drink. Luckily there were some cans of Coors Light in the fridge and a half gallon of pink lemonade to mix in. Rather, some Rocky Mountain Rosé as my buddy Joel calls it. So we crack into one and then another as her and her friend— whose place we both stayed(though I didn't remember her name at the time)—start pulling out photo strips from the bar where apparently I met them the night before. One is of me and Lara sloppily making out through laughter. I have zero recollection of the moment as I'm inspecting the strip, but there's no denying it happened. Without thinking I put it in my jacket pocket like a time bomb my subconscious made sure to plant and we carry on with the other photos.

Meanwhile, Aubrey texts: "Where are you?"

I admit the truth with certain omissions, and she's concerned—naturally. The weekends have always been

sacred to us. Both of us being career oriented with de-
manding jobs and alternating schedules meant that our
weeknights were just a matter of hours. Long enough to
walk our dogs, have a few drinks, eat dinner, and go to
bed. The weekends we were inseparable. And this particular Sunday we had planned on doing nothing but watch
movies in bed, order in, and have casual drinks as our
little pups cuddled us sweetly. She was wondering if I was
still coming.

I responded: "Yes. I'm leaving now. Should be there
in 15."

But cars are harder to call than you'd think on Sunday mornings in Glassell Park. The car itself will be here
in 15 minutes I mention to the girls and they're surprised
at the news. Not the wait time, but that I'm leaving. I
don't want to offend anyone, so I cancel the car and make
a drink while suggesting a smoke out front.

The hill on which the apartment is located is outra-
geous, on such a steep angle that it forces one to lean back
considerably while walking downhill like a comical star
out of a silent film. When what is now my second car arrives, it pulls over to the curb a few buildings down. I stub
out my smoke, finish my drink, say goodbye to the girls,
then exaggerate the aforementioned Chaplin-esque walk
in my approach to the car...that suddenly pulls away
from the curb and speeds off. Fair enough. Had I seen me
Chaplin'ing down the hill in my rearview mirror I would
have driven off too. People were still in morning mass for
fuck's sake. I'll even pay the $5 cancellation fee without
any qualms.

By the time I make it to Aubrey it's close to noon and
she's clearly upset—as she should be. Though nothing

happened, *it's completely beside the point*. What must have occurred in her brain was a nightmare. A disaster. A fucking orgy. What a sad thought. Disgusting even…*and reckless as hell*.

We briefly discuss the previous evening over a drink in the kitchen and I soothe her worries. We're able to move past it and enjoy our Sunday exactly as planned, ending it in bed with our dogs after dinner while a movie plays. She falls asleep before me. I look at her and my heart swells and eyes fill with tears. I sidle up next to her and wrap my arm tightly around her. Her heartbeat is steady and strong. She snores very quietly. Even more quietly, I whisper, "I'm sorry." And as I close my eyes I wonder—could this still work?

"So this must've been where you were Saturday night?" The time bomb in my jacket pocket went off. It's Monday morning and she's tossing the photo strip of me and Lara onto the bed next to me. She's crying. It's devastating—

She's crying and now I'm crying too, the tears streaming down my face as I finish my final sprint at 100% and ease into a walk. No longer in Portland. No longer in my head in Aubrey's bed on that Monday morning three weeks ago. Just weak legged and teary eyed on a sidewalk in Koreatown, a fucking mess for all of 6th Street traffic to see in passing—oh boy. What the fuck is happening. A deep breath, hands held on the back of my head. I need to get cleaned up.

Back at my place, the urge to get cleaned up expands outside of myself and into the apartment where I first wash all of the dishes and clean the floors—for an hour. Then I pour a glass of rosé, go into the bathroom and cut off all my long, wavy hair, shave my six week beard, and take a shower. The effect is less than desirable, but it's a start. Rather than looking like a young man with his whole life ahead of him I look like a high school baseball coach. The one that won't just buy you beer, but will drink it with you at the party and probably hit on your girlfriend. A real fucking scumbag. Which is perhaps appropriate anyway.

Afterwards it strikes me that the place needs more than a cleaning. It needs a deep cleaning, on hands and knees, and to be rearranged completely. For a studio apartment I've accumulated a fair amount of furniture. From working at the Galerie I've come into a desk, a bookshelf, a metal table used as a bar, a round kitchen table, a few stools, a daybed, three heavy white marble slabs that are used as a coffee table, as well as a long, 4-seater sofa that belongs in a place much larger than this one. Still, with careful consideration I've brought these things into my home knowing that each piece will fit in a very specific spot in my floorplan and I have to say that it's all come together quite nicely. But now it's a disaster as I'm pulling and scooting everything around, trying the furniture every which way in an attempt to reshape my surroundings until eventually it's all in a heap in the middle of the room and I'm exhausted and sweating like this was actually the final sprint in my jog from earlier.

Frustrated, I sit down on the wooden frame of the daybed and recline as I stare at the mattress thrown haphazardly onto the sofa. None of it makes sense anywhere but where it was. None of this makes any sense. Again, I think back to that Monday morning three weeks ago.

Through tears: "Why do you even still hang out with me?"

It was a pointed question given the circumstances, and there wasn't time to give the deserved answer at length. In truth, because I still love you. I don't know what's wrong with me, though I'm starting to figure some of that out. I was 23 when we met, and completely unprepared. I have unresolved issues with sex for reasons I've touched on previously, including being molested and growing up within a set of Christian ideals. Though I hate to admit it, I very much have an ego and am in constant need of validation. I'm deeply unhappy with my career because unfortunately accomplishment is not synonymous with success. And your issues compounded my own, which has resulted in our love becoming a disaster much like this heap of furniture currently piled in the middle of my apartment. Not that these are good excuses, or excuses at all. But they're valid talking points meant for intimate discussion, and instead of talking them through I left…and as I lay here now I realize that as much as a change is desired, sometimes the situation simply doesn't permit it.

With a sigh, I realize that the work I've put in has to be reversed. Everything must get put back into its proper place because it doesn't work elsewhere. The metaphor is not lost on me, but it does require another glass of rosé to digest. And then another to keep moving.

By the time I get the apartment back in order it's 8.15pm and I'm lonely as hell, the endorphins from the workout having worn off and the rosé having settled in. I sit on the bed, made neatly with fresh sheets, and I contemplate re-downloading *Kindling*. The urge is unbearable. *It is time to change.* Maybe I'll switch to *Ramble*. Change is good, even if it's small. This is a step in the right direction—right? Fuck. Another glass of rosé and my phone dings twice. I jump pathetically at the possibility of even the tiniest bit of validation.

It's another text, this time from my dad: "If your kid someday asks you, 'What was your dad like?' (assuming I'm already dead), what would you tell him/her?"

Oh, what the fuck. I respond: "He was a badass. Let's start at he was a Puerto Rican kid from Jersey City who was fluent in Mandarin. Only gets better from there."

Then 29 minutes later, I respond again: "You feeling dark? What's up?"

Dad: "I worry that I contributed to YOUR darkness."

Me: "Damn man. You been going to therapy or something?"

Dad: "No. Just worry about my baby boy."

Me: "I appreciate it, but I'm alright. Always will be."

Dad: "We're all damaged."

Me: "Don't I know it!"

Dad: "I miss you"

Me: "I miss you too."

And I miss her too. Terribly. If you're listening, I miss You. I miss you so fucking much. If any of you are listening—truly, anyone—I miss you as well. And thank you. As I said before, *I'm really fucking scared to go into this shit alone.* Your presence is invaluable to my survival and will never go unappreciated. I'm here for you too.

Now, I know it's early, but let's go to bed. Please, lay down. I'll put some music on and pour one last glass. We won't have to say another word til morning....

VIII

GUNSHOTS RING OUT IN THE DARK PRE-DAWN, waking us in our warm bed as a gentle rain falls in the Tuscan countryside. It's the first day of wild boar season and the hunters are out early, methodically taking their shots at what feels to be evenly spaced intervals—musical somehow.

We listen as we make love, the sun slowly rising somewhere within the clouds creating an even blue glow in our room in the villa. We can hear your family walking around the house and smell the coffee and breakfast from the kitchen downstairs as Sylvia the cook prepares it with a warm smile, but we are careful to not set off any alarm. Our words are whispered, our moans are subdued, quieted by a palm that is then bitten. Your deep brown eyes stare into mine, the pupils dilated in the dark, and in love. It's everything.

I love you still at breakfast as you pour our champagne aggressively taller than anyone else's, then butter your toast with equal enthusiasm before slopping on the jam. I love the way you eat on vacation. I love the way you drink on vacation. I love the way you fuck on vacation.

How do you suspend these moments? How do you stretch and bend this bright light so it reaches inside the tunnels and illuminates the darkness? How do you bottle it and carry it forth as a lantern as you descend into this shit?

This was already almost a year ago, but I remember it well. It was the 13th of October—your birthday.

In the afternoon the rain has picked up into a steady downpour accompanied by thunder. We watch with wine from the window nook off the stairs to the attic, then suddenly we're down in it—

In our hooded yellow slickers that go down to our shins we walk through the trees until we get to a bright green clearing in the lawn. Out of sight from your family as they stoke the fire inside, we have a smoke and stand closely, not ever wanting to be apart again. Your brother and his girlfriend come down, not to join or to judge, but to simply enjoy this moment as well. They snap a picture of us from behind, the plumes of smoke from our cigarettes passing as our breath in the cold rain. It's still the background on my phone.

It rings later on when we're all huddled inside with food and drinks and a card game. It's the gate to the property, informing me of a delivery that confuses you greatly.

You had forgotten your book on the flight from LA. It was devastating. You had been so excited to read it, so I had a copy overnighted to the villa, which somehow arrived through the muddy country roads to our remote location in time for your birthday. You were elated when I returned inside and you opened the package. I had done something right. You whispered I love you. Everything was alright. We could have been OK.

If only it were all in a bottle, glowing in this darkness to help me find my way. Instead, it's in a bright neon sign: Cocktails. Flashing in red, ominous yet still optimistic at any prospect of relief.

I had been at my buddy's play earlier, having attended by myself even though I had bought two tickets.

Afterwards a polite three drinks were had in the lobby for small talk and congratulations and eventually I called a Lyft to head home. En route, the idea of walking through the door into my empty apartment without you or the pups became overwhelming. I thought it might be best if I stop for one last drink out, so here I am.

And what the fuck am I doing? The bar is a narrow eight feet wide dive that stretches deep into the back past a pool table that barely fits and in to two bathrooms whose white painted doors are filthy with smudges from unwashed hands. The clientele is a bizarre mix of a hip, urban crowd, couples in their mid 50's on double dates to play darts, and legitimate local drunks. Then me. And although I can see how my presence at the bar makes sense and is just as dumb and cliché as anything else, I can't stand it anymore so I slam my drink and walk out.

One block down a homeless man appears in front of me, loud and violent, and very incoherent. I step back in shock, "Sorry?"

But the small, wide eyed man steps towards me again with a strange swing of the arms and more incoherent yelling. After I take another few steps back he just stands there mumbling, and I don't know what he's doing, but I want nothing of it so step into the street and walk quickly by. Back on the sidewalk, I take one last confused look back at him and the light catches the blade of a 7-inch butcher's knife in his right hand. Incredible. I freeze, noting that there's a woman standing at the bus stop 20 feet on the other side of him. I try to gesture for her to stay away, mouthing *he's got a knife* as suddenly my gesture turns into a stabbing motion as if that's going to help put this woman at ease or make her any safer. She doesn't understand—shit.

Swinging wide back out into the street past the guy, then over to the bus stop I approach her. "He's got a knife. I was just trying to say stay away."

She's in her 50's with kind eyes and a distracting, thick grey streak in the middle of her dark curly hair. "I know. You reacted better than I did. I just froze."

"Wait, you saw it?"

"I was just sitting on the bench waiting for the bus and he came up behind me and put it in my face. I didn't know what to do, so I didn't move. You reacted better than I did."

"Jesus. Do I call 911?"

"I don't know. I'm just waiting for my bus to go home."

"Fuck. Alright. I'm calling 911." And I do, but when the operator finally comes on the line she's deeply disappointed in me.

"If he's got a knife, what are you still doing there? Leave." You degenerate good Samaritan, get the fuck out.

I try to explain about the woman at the bus stop and the passersby on the sidewalk and how the man could very well stab any one of them if I weren't here to protect or redirect their foot traffic.

She explains, "He could stab you too. You need to leave now." Then hangs up with the promise of sending a squad car.

By the time the two squad cars arrive I still haven't learned the woman's name who's waiting for her bus, which has yet to arrive. We watch the police investigate the homeless man, then quickly leave him alone in the vestibule that he's claimed as his own. Finally, her bus comes. She thanks me and climbs aboard, then disappears forever. Not dead, but no longer a living part of my life either. It strikes me as a lonely thought.

As I head back home, I'm compelled to stop and talk to the two officers, mentioning that I'm the one who called them in the first place.

"Yeah, we found the knife. A pocket knife. Don't think he means any trouble."

"A pocket knife?" I question, like a real nosey motherfucker.

"Yeah, a pocket knife. These homeless folk get really possessive over their territory. He's harmless."

"Right, no…but you didn't find another knife on him? It was huge."

"Another knife? No. We found a pocket knife. What did you see? Was it retractable, or a fixed blade?"

"It was a fixed blade, like 7-inches long." I'm subdued, but incredulous. No shit you ask to see a knife and he presents you with a tiny pocket knife, which actually terrifies me more because it means he's of sound enough mind to conceal the big one. "He's got a butcher's knife. Ask him again."

The last drink alone after the play may have left me with the smell of booze, and I'm deeply upset with myself by this fact. It doesn't matter. The cops probably don't give a fuck anyway. As if this is their biggest call of the night?

They've got my name and number and as I walk away I get angrier with each step. Not at them or at anyone in particular, but at the fact that this is the world we live in. Had I reacted differently—had I reacted at all—that strange swiping motion of the homeless man's hands could've been a stabbing one right into my guts, and then what?

All of this comes right after an incident in the alley behind the Galerie where I work, 10am on a Friday. I was working inside the warehouse on my computer, listening to far too calm music on my headphones when John the head mover storms in with an excited story relayed secondarily to me, but primarily to someone he's on the phone with as he gestures for me to listen to the details as well:

"Yeah, so when we pull up Sydnie is arguing with the guy already and she motions for me to block him in with the truck. Then Allen gets out and approaches the guy as he's yelling at Sydnie and then the guy shoves Allen, so David runs over and starts talking shit and the guy takes a swing at him, but I run in and break it up and shove the guy onto his car and talk everyone down. Apparently it all started because this guy decided to park his car and just take a piss right there in the parking lot and Sydnie saw him out of her office window and ran down and started screaming at the guy. Anyway—"

And he goes on similarly in this sort of strange calm manner, very pleased with the event whose details become a little unclear, but which ultimately ends with the guy getting back into his car and threatening to shoot Allen, who pokes his head into the man's window and eggs him on with, "Oh you're gonna shoot me?"

The guy removes a pistol and some bullets and fumbles to load it while Allen starts filming him on his phone. "You got a gun? You gonna shoot me? You gonna shoot me?"

The guy doesn't shoot him. He drops the bullets as he swipes at Allen's phone and knocks it to the ground. When Allen goes to pick it up the guy manages to punch him in the neck and then speed away. Able to pick up his phone and start recording again, Allen captures the make, model, and license plate of the car. The police are called and respond accordingly. Everyone is interviewed at length and the license plate is called in. A name and address are quickly acquired. All from the safety of our own alley parking lot at the Galerie storage. Then we get back to work like nothing happened, including Allen though it's apparent something did happen from his bright red, swollen neck.

Two weeks later when I'm walking lunch down the very same alley to the same movers that are working in our storage space, this memory should cause more apprehension than it does when I see an argument 100 yards ahead. It doesn't matter, I can just walk right through it. Twenty or so people in heated argument, I'm sure it's fine. The guys are hungry. I'll just walk right through it and get them their lunch.

Now 50 yards away from the brawl I become uneasy when I hear racial slurs and N-bombs being hurled from each side, which I now realize is about 10 on 10 with one side being black kids in their young 20's and the other side being older Armenian guys—fuck. Do I really want to take the chance at being some white guy innocently entering what could be a racially charged altercation? I stop dead in my tracks, everyone's lunch getting colder by the second in the to-go bags I hold helpless in my hands. What a perfect view I have of the paunchy Armenian man's attempt at a round house kick to one of the kid's faces—Jesus! Missing, of course, but recovering quickly to grab a broom handle and returning to the kid with a lofty swing that breaks the broom handle over the kid's face—oh, what the fuck? Nope. I turn on my heels to make a B-line back to the main Galerie and as I do so a gunshot rings out. Not the peaceable one of wild boar season in the Tuscan countryside, but one of the city that is quickly accompanied by screaming.

Running back inside Galerie, I lock the metal screen door behind me as two of the kids sprint away from the scene, one calling back to the other, "Fuck no, man! He might be dead!"

I'm trembling as I call 911 for the second time this month and receive a busy signal. Then connect on the second try and attempt to recount the events with a quaking voice, taking way too long to get out the words, "There was a gun shot. I think someone got shot."

Within 30 seconds a police helicopter is circling the alley and squad cars are pulling up. No one is in sight. No bodies on the ground. It's quiet aside from the roar of the helicopter circling overhead.

For the next three hours the alley is taped off and no one is allowed access. The helicopter has disappeared, but it's droning whir remains in my ears, beating in the gradually slowing rhythm of my heart. Have I been so emboldened by the luxury of this flimsy, pallid bubble to think that it couldn't happen to me? Have I been so blinded?

It's all catching up, closing in. Too close now. 50 yards to be exact. The knife, the gun, the gun shot. A man took his wife and daughters hostage, eventually releasing them before taking his own life. A 27 year old kid was shot to death blocks down outside of a bar called The Pit, where Aubrey and I once had our first date. Another 27 year old kid threw himself off a four story apartment building to his death. Everywhere is either under water, under attack, on fire, or simply crumbling. And then there's the fact of our president. Our country. Irreparable damage—et al. What the fuck.

Yet with all of that, still the most devastating news to report today is that it's now your birthday and I won't be there to celebrate it. I don't even know where you are. So Officially: Happy Birthday, Aubrey. Hope you enjoy it and celebrate. We may not be together, but I'm happy as hell you're out there somewhere.

You respond with a drunken text: "The first one to wish me a happy birthday and the only person I wish I were spending it with."

Christ. I miss you every second. I just never want to make things worse or more painful. That's why I typically resist the urge to text you, but tonight was too much.

My light is on for you—always. I love you more than anything and I'll never stop.

IX

THE NUMBNESS BEGINS IN MY FEET then shoots up my legs and into my chest with a wave of panic that rattles through my teeth. A heart palpitation. I'm dying. Then nothing.

It occurred to me that you, kind and patient reader, may feel mislead. That was never my intention. What began as A Self-Help Book About Anxiety has spun, maybe wildly, into somewhat of a larger yarn, and if you'd like we can use it all to knit you a nice sweater as an apology gift. Please though, let it be clear that the anxiety has not simply gone away. The purpose of this book remains clear, but there's no way of resolving the issue without first addressing what's beneath it.

Existence, sure. And the idea of non-existence and what it all means, etc. etc. Self-medicating. Sex. Self-worth. The need for constant validation. Again, self-medicating. And the multitude of issues that arise in a cyclical and acutely annoying pattern. If you find yourself frustrated, you are not alone in that frustration. And if you must, please make a brief return to the Disclaimer of this book which very openly admits to me, the writer, being more desperate for this book than anyone.

The numbness is new though. It would seem in this mad spiral that my anxiety has recently developed a novel and exciting way of manifesting itself, which involves much more than just the brain but that *complicated minutiae of the body* that includes the organs and the nervous system itself. It's no longer just the brain backfiring. It's your sweet little temple telling you you've done fucked up. Yes—you've done fucked up bad. But let's not get off track again. At least not yet. Let us sit for a moment with this notion of Numbness.

Definition: the state of being numb. OK then, **Numb**: *adjective* 1. Deprived of the power of sensation. 2. Unable to think, feel, or respond normally. *Verb* 1. Deprive of feeling or responsiveness. 2. Cause (a sensation) to be felt less intensely; deaden.

Upon further consideration, *numbness* might not be the best word to describe the sensation I've been experiencing. Maybe a precursor to it, but the actual sensation itself might be better described as an intense tingling that begins in the feet, then shoots up into the legs and heart. Like every feeling I've been avoiding suddenly hits at once in an overwhelming systemic attack on myself.

It's incredible what the body is capable of. With little distinction between good and bad, healthy or unhealthy, it absorbs everything until it reaches capacity. And it either bottles up and explodes or it reaches its boiling point and a valve opens somewhere to expel piping hot steam that will burn the shit out of you. Is there an in between? I used to relate to the former, but this new tingling would have to situate me firmly under the latter. Out of nowhere, short and fast and hot as fuck. Which is perhaps more terrifying, because although intense and short lived it comes with the knowledge that the body has been breaking itself down below the surface all the while. The painful blast of steam just happens to be the only tangible evidence recognized by the untrained eye while a doctor would probably have the insight to tell you of a far greater harm—ulcers, high blood pressure, cancer, et al. But there's no time to think about all that in the present, as a trip to WebMD would lead only to more numbness, more tingling, and sheer prolonged panic.

It's incredible what the mind is capable of too. In the same way that the physical symptoms of this disease(I do stress that word) that 1 out of 5 Americans are afflicted by finds means of escape, so do the accompanying mental and creative ones. Maybe a touch more productive and legitimately cathartic, but they are no less annoying.

For instance, amidst all of this incredible nonsense I have managed to start a country band. Did I not tell you? Cain and I formed it back in July and it's only mostly fake. It's called Sad As Hell. Our first album is called Dark Country and there's a very real chance that you'll never hear it because it will never be made. However, some of the songs do exist on paper. I'll sing you one now:

How are we broken up.
How are we broken so much.
That all we can talk about
Is how we're broken by touch.

My skin is a fragile film
That no one can star in
Except you and your friends
When the audience goes on a binge.

They're looking for something
That we'll never give.
Hope is a burden,
And optimism's too hard in the end.

We're flighty, but stuck
Up to our necks in sand
But our thoughts so far above.
Don't chase em unless you're ready
For the ground.

How will we ever wake up.
How will we wake to talk.
About how we're broken
And how much we're fucked up.

My tears form a fragile film
Over my eyes and then
I remember you and your friends
And all the shit we're caught up in.

We're looking for something
That we'll never get.
Hope is a burden,
But optimism is the drug to stick in.

How are we broken up.
How are we broken this much.
That our last hope is in the bottle.
The whole model is just broken and fucked.

Don't mind the fact that I can't write a hook. Or that I can't play any instruments and certainly can't sing. Especially when the most telling aspect of this nonexistent band is that their last song—written back in July—was never completed. It simply starts and then ends in three little lines:

This is the end, I can feel it coming on.
My lips are numb and my pulse is gone.
Honey, take the wheel—

Fuck.

But let us steer ourselves in yet another direction, towards a destination that promises a cookbook. Cooking is a cathartic exercise to say the least, which I thoroughly enjoy and have begun doing again. It is only natural that I should want to combine this discipline with that of writing and I have arrived at a logical title for this cookbook: *Meals For One*.

The first recipe is one that I call "The Ruffoli," which is called as such because it is the last name of the people whose home I first witnessed this meal being cooked. An idyllic vision of an American household of four, it was the housekeeper/chef who was preparing the meal. I only happened to bear witness to this vision because I was installing a light fixture in their kitchen as the meal was being prepared and experienced an overwhelming yet vague feeling of homesickness as a result. Of course, I've put my own spin on this delicacy, which I will illustrate now:

The Ruffoli

Ingredients
1lb ground turkey
1 sweet onion, diced
5 cloves of garlic, minced
1 zucchini, cubed
3 handfuls of shredded kale
½ package of shredded mozzarella

First, begin by pouring yourself a glass of wine, taking a sip, and putting on melancholy music. Then remove your tiny wooden cutting board that has nearly split in two, but hangs by a thread. Then take out your knife, which now lacks a handle and operates more as an over-sized razorblade. Now preheat your single pan on medium heat while you very quickly and skillfully dice the onion using a trick your friend taught you nearly ten years ago from his culinary school days. Put a spoonful of coconut oil in the pan, which is now preheated, then dump in the onion and lightly salt to aid in the caramelization process. Shake the pan and light a cigarette.

For half a cigarette let the onion cook, then turn the heat to low while you mince the garlic, cube the zucchini, and finish your cigarette. Pour another glass of wine too. Yours is empty.

Take the onion off the heat and set aside in the large mixing bowl from the set of your parents' wedding china, then return the pan to the heat and turn it back to medium. Another spoonful of coconut oil with a few tears. Put in the garlic for a moment or two of sadness, then follow with all of the ground turkey. Wash your hands. Then comes the salt, pepper, garlic powder, onion powder, a touch of cayenne. Stir with a wooden spoon as you light a second cigarette.

Once the cigarette is stubbed out and the glass of wine gone, the ground turkey will be perfectly browned. Remove it from the heat and put it in the bowl with the onion. Return the pan to the heat. More coconut oil. Then drop in the zucchini, lightly salted. Careful not to overcook. Maybe ten deep breaths to resist the urge to cry. Then return the ground turkey, onion, and garlic mixture to the pan. Mix together. Then add the kale to the top with a touch more salt, more garlic powder, more onion powder, and a few splashes of balsamic vinegar to help the kale soften more quickly. Keep mixing everything together to numb the pain.

Soon enough the kale will wilt and you'll turn the heat to low. As you sprinkle all of the mozzarella over the top you realize that you might not actually be hungry and this whole cooking operation has been yet another creative distraction to keep your mind off your anxiety and loneliness. It is imperative to turn the heat to low at this point and cover with a lid. It is time for another cigarette and another glass of wine. This time at the window where you will experience a profound sadness over your circumstances. This is far too much food. Will you always be alone, cooking for one? You miss your Someone. You miss who you were when you were with them. Have a good cry.

Before you know it, the cigarette is gone and you slam the rest of the glass of wine. The food is ready. You should probably eat. Serve a moderate portion in a small bowl from your parents' wedding china. Pour another glass. Return the lid to the pan, turn off the heat, and go sit on your bed to enjoy your meal with a movie.

Total cook/prep time: 3 cigarettes, 4 glasses of wine, and 1 good cry

For reheating: in the same pan which you refrigerated overnight(or perhaps left out and then refrigerated in the morning), simply turn the heat to medium low for 1 cigarette and 2 glasses of wine, then serve and enjoy with another movie and very good cry. For the next three nights. Bon appétit.

Indeed, a man does have to eat. Regardless of your emotional state, it is necessary to provide your body with enough nourishment to continue to exist. Even if your mind and heart tell you you're not hungry, you need to eat. This may be a distraction, but it is perhaps the most important and healthiest one I've discovered in my battle against anxiety.

Inversely, steering in a completely terrifying direction now, I will admit that one of my newest distractions has come by way of contemplating doing stand-up, which might be the unhealthiest of these diversions. Comedians: the most tragic of artists. I'd provide evidence if I felt it necessary, but I believe this statement comes as a simple fact. Scary then to have begun to fantasize of my own stand-up routine, which I only put down now for the sake of science. We are scientists then. This is a study:

The stage is small and the venue itself is intimate. The lights are low. A spotlight illuminates the mic, which I approach in a casual and subdued demeanor which borders on "sullen" or even "down and out" and is accompanied by a very gentle, soothing voice.

"Anyone ever dated a hypothermic? They're chill at first, then just downright frigid."

Pause for laughter. It doesn't come, naturally. But continue to pause for just a touch too long.

"I'm kidding. Can you imagine? I just come out here with a 10 minute set of puns? Jesus. I could see all your assholes clenching. Y'all raised a fucking inch off your seats."

Mimic an asshole clenching by way of tightening your fist with the anal-like meeting of thumb and index finger facing the audience while straightening your posture to become an inch or two taller.

"No. No. But dating's a fucking nightmare. Has anyone ever tried online dating?" (Several people raise their hands, but don't even consider them.) "What about a threesome? Has anyone ever had a threesome?"

Maybe an awkward hand or two, but this isn't about them. Continue:

"I have. Two actually. The first when I was 18, in my friend's basement. My buddy and I were hanging out with one of our really good friends, and she was a virgin. She wanted to lose it to us, which at 18 sounds pretty fucking badass. Not to mention I'd been reading some Beatnik shit that talked about 'Yab-Yum'—you ever heard of that?"

A few people have, but give a basic and idiotic explanation of what you thought it was:

"Yab-Yum, so I thought, was basically this spiritual/sexual practice of a woman playing mother and caregiver to the men she loved. But still, sexual. So when you break it down it sounds creepy as shit…but when you're 18 you're just thinking this is beautiful and we all love each other, so yeah let's light candles and provide for each other. And drink vodka first. Lots of vodka. That's definitely a part of the spiritual process. Let's do this.

"So we did all that and there was music playing and everything seemed right—for them. I was nervous. Was Yab-Yum real? What the fuck was happening? While they started I drank more vodka, as you do. Then took a deep breath when she told me she wanted me to join—"

Take a drink. A deep pull. Then a long breath.

"Straight men. Have you ever had a man shove his dick in your face? Don't be shy. There's no shame in it. I just need to know if I'm alone in this story from here on out. You ever had a dick shoved in your face?"

Everyone's really uncomfortable. Their assholes are definitely tightening. Everyone's rising an inch off their seats.

"Well I have. And the second he put it in my face I realized that this was the last thing I wanted to be doing in the world, so quickly put on my clothes and walked upstairs and out into the lawn and puked…then went for a 6 mile walk at two in the morning. Threesomes are great. Badass. The second one was actually better. Happened just a few weeks ago. Like I said, dating is a nightmare…but sometimes it's a beautiful one."

Another swig. Slight reconsideration of the facts. Some awkwardness.

"Alright, truth be told I might need an audience vote to see if this second one really qualifies as a threesome. A raise of hands: is it considered a threesome if you jerk off with one woman's panties around your face and another woman's panties in your mouth? Neither is in the room or even knows you're doing it just then, but they did volunteer their panties on two very separate prior occasions. Does that count as a threesome? A show of hands please."

Well…I didn't realize this very small room's audience, who I can make direct eye contact with despite the low lights, could get even more uncomfortable. Does your drink really need to be stirred again? Is your boyfriend's elbow *that* interesting? Fine. We'll move on.

"I'm kidding. Again. Jesus! Of course it doesn't count. I'm kidding, I'm kidding. Can you imagine?"

Laugh awkwardly. You may not have been kidding. Either way, they *Can* imagine.

"So weird. If I just got up here and like shot off a pun and then got straight into my masturbating habits? Weird as fuck."

The audience definitely agrees that it's weird as fuck.

"I wasn't kidding about dating though. It's a fucking nightmare. Who here has tried online dating? I know I already asked, but I wasn't actually looking to see if anyone raised their hands, I was more just wondering if anyone had had a threesome. So who here has tried online dating?"

The same people as before raise their hands. This time they're considered.

"It's insane, right? I feel like it accelerates the process. There's no courting anymore. Now you both just swipe right according to a few pictures and a tiny bio and suddenly you're an item. You're dating. How? And you run the course of an entire relationship in a matter of weeks. For me personally, I've been in a series of explosive two week relationships. That seems to be the norm…for the version of you or them that's been presented to be broken down into the reality of things in just two weeks and then one of you steps back like, 'What the fuck?' and then disappears. No matter how good your intentions, the whole thing is set up for failure. Also, why wouldn't it be? Do they make money off you meeting The One, or do they make it off you deleting the app and re-downloading it over and over because of certain failure? Fuck, dating's a nightmare…."

From here the "stand-up" routine actually becomes a full-on rant on the experience, but it is in everyone's best interest that we not get into that for now. I need to catch my breath. There's tingling in my feet…and it's shooting up through my legs and into my chest. I need to sit down.

I'm not dying.… I just need a moment, then we can get back to it. And maybe in the third person would be more fun. Yes. Your writer, he will be right back.

X

THE POOR MAN HAD CONVINCED HIMSELF a shot of rosé each morning was a salubrious action and that wine was good for the heart. It was certainly the simpler way to think about it, rather than admitting that it might be problematic. AA—what a nightmare! The Europeans did it all the time anyway.

This was not the only European approach he took to life. He had adopted their way of thinking romantically too. Big love. Broad and free. He had never actually dated before—only been in one long relationship after the next—so getting out there would be healthy. Very good for the heart. But, as his track record would suggest, he was not particularly skilled in the art of Casual. This led to many complications and a dizzying series of explosive two week relationships.

The first was back in July, which the man himself once referenced using the terms of a parking lot, describing the days as if they were parking spots J1, J2, J3, J4, and so on. Perhaps not the most delicate terms to use while speaking of a romantic affair, but they reflected a desperate attempt to find the humor in heartbreak, and he did have good intentions. Then again, just because you have good intentions doesn't mean you can't very quickly fuck things up.

July was disastrous, like a tropical storm by the name of "Lara." She had picked up force in the deep gulf of a break up two months prior before finally hitting his shores as a certified hurricane that would cause great devastation. After two years together with her ex, the break up was said to have been caused by her cat. They were finally moving in together and she was informed that the cat could not join. Absolutely not. Of course, no break up has ever been caused by a cat alone, and this poor little creature must have been the scapegoat for a myriad of other underlying issues—much simpler to blame the cat. Still, Lara's arms flailed about as the winds picked up and tears beat down like hard rain that promised to wreak havoc.

Hurricane Lara. A Category "5 Months of Free Pussy" as she crudely put it herself at a diner table over French fries in the wild night of J1. She was crass, yet sensitive in her own right, a direct and rather lanky girl from Fresno who had been homeschooled all her life. Perhaps one of the reasons her social skills were skewed, though not without their own unique charm, and this not taking into account her emotional unavailability at the time. She had been quite fond of the phrase, "I don't give a fuck," as well as telling the man to, "Get over [himself]!"

With each repetition of this latter phrase the man was stirred more deeply and the waves crashed against his vitals more and more vigorously until the walls could no longer bear the burden. How could he get over himself when he believed to have never been under or into himself? For years he had accommodated the needs of another person, essentially adopting their life while hardly hanging onto a shred of his own. And here he was repeating this pattern: listening to the details of Lara's ex-boyfriend woes, drying her tears, helping her find a new apartment for her and her cat, et cetera, without any reciprocation. He was again getting lost, and upon recognizing such decided to cash out on the 5 Month Voucher and simply walk away after a matter of weeks.

As the waters began to calm, he found himself inexplicably wearing all white as he sailed upon the sea on a journey to see a woman named Alice. A strange, emotional detail of his voyage was kept in a logbook, which is presented here in part to illustrate his state of mind, and maybe even to suggest that he was losing it:

J20/17, 10.10pm
Don't be annoyed, but feel free to roll your eyes. It's insane. This is about insanity when it comes down to it. Love. That's what it is, by the way. Specialists admit that it's a mental state where everything either fails to take shape or falls perfectly into place. Here.

And don't be scared either. But do be prepared for your heart to flutter and to let your eyes water. There it is. You just texted me your eyes, pretty and wide and wet. At this hour and in only so many days? Reminder: this is insane.

This isn't a prank, or a trick, or anything like a certain aforementioned masturbatory fuck. It's not "a bowl of oranges" for that matter either. It just is. If I could draw you, I would. Right here, right now:

[A messy circle is drawn onto the page. Nothing more.]

But I clearly can't draw for shit and I'm beginning to write sloppily and make errors. I guess it's time to quit for the night. Alone with rosé at the end of a long day. I wish you were here.

Then finally, my response: "My girl."

xo

J21/17, 9.30am
Perhaps a bit too much of the rosé last night. I don't know. Maybe it's getting out of hand. Everything seems to be going that direction. I'm losing control. Or maybe for the first time I'm just fully allowing the tides to take me. All my decisions have been made. I built the goddamn boat, put it in the water, and climbed in. Let's see where I end up.

I haven't re-read anything from last night. I'll do my best to keep it that way. I have to get to work now. You were the last thought I had before bed and the first upon waking. Today marks the 6th day with you in my life. Oh dear….

I should put on pants and get above deck.

xo

J21/17, 11.14pm
There must be something about the chemistry of the body in connection with your proximity to another, the quality, and for what length of time. The way the body's chemicals change, and the brain's. I'm having trouble adapting to your absence as if suffering from withdrawals. We've known each other less than a week, yet I feel sick and am

experiencing mild confusion and an inability to focus throughout the day. It's terrifying.

Moreover, I'm experiencing an acute sense of discomfort that I can only attribute to my own fears and self-doubt that feels much like nausea. I could very well throw up at the ideas my awful imagination creates while we're apart. The images themselves aren't worth delving into, and the subject itself I care not to mention further than you had to go to bed early tonight from feeling ill—but what if you felt fine and simply didn't want to feel obligated to text me after a certain hour? You had your own business to tend to. You had other people to whom you would prefer to devote your time. Am I really that needy? Do I really lack that much confidence that I require constant reassurance? I promised you a goodnight picture, which I sent…of me here with my wine, poised to write this very entry. A large part of me had hoped to receive the same from you. A goodnight picture of you at your hotel, alone. Of course, it didn't come, most likely because you felt ill and like you didn't look your best(I'm sure you did, you're always beautiful). Yet still my mind wandered— are you alone? Right now, are you dreaming of the day we're together again? I can't bear the alternative. It's too miserable. And what does that say about me, and my own patterns of behavior?

I will not self-destruct. Not this time. I will not act out over some abstract rejection for self-preservation or otherwise. I will not ruin something good because my mind wanders and my heart gets heavy with possibility. Instead, I will finish this entry. I will finish this rosé. I will make a small plate of leftovers and go to bed.

I'm not a child. Despite the logic and optimism. Despite the abandonment of logic and blind faith in the optimism. But I'll love you like one. With innocence and complete devotion.

Yours, forever. Or until you want to throw me overboard. With love and love and love.

xo

J22/17, 10.37am
How quickly things can change. Or rather, in the words of Dinah Washington: "What a difference a day can make. 24 little hours…." Or 12. Hell, 5 even. How quickly all self-doubt and weakness can be alleviated. And how easily.

Five hours after I sign off here you send a text, at a bright and early 7.17am your time: "Good morning from the world's worst hotel."

It accompanies a picture of you in bed, the white sheets wrapped around your fair skin, a hint of thigh, shoulders bare—I want to kiss them. Your mouth parted slightly in a tiny smile—I need to kiss it. Your hair has the perfect amount of mess—I want to run my fingers through it. And your eyes, impossible in size and brightness and color— I'm staring into them…and everything else washes away as I feel you staring back. You took this for me. A special moment shared across the ocean. Ours alone. And it's perfect. Thank you.

xo

J22/17, 2.45pm
What a difference a day can make. How quickly things can change. In one little hour. One little error. But we'll get to that.

I floated, high as hell, all day in a dream. Your affection feeding me all the right combination of pills. No numbness, quite the opposite. Body tingling head to toe. Your every word the right movement on my skin, crawling...tightening—whatever. I was fucking high as hell, lucid...in a dream...on the wall of a dim lit restaurant where you sat at a table by yourself, drinking wine and reading my book. You weren't looking for yourself in there, skimming pages looking for names that start with A—you were just reading, diving into my Self.

Am I fucking drunk right now? I got very little sleep last night. I was up til 6am somewhere between sadness, frustration, and anger. Certainly tears were involved, you know. Because what the fuck happened? You asked for something and didn't like what you found?

Jesus. I'm just now realizing the full extent of it. Picture this: my stomach didn't hurt at the moment, it actually felt quite good, yet still you asked me to climb on the table so you could take a look. You cut in and asked, "Okay, what happens? How do you act out?"

Reminder: my stomach didn't hurt just then, but you still pulled it all out...because, upon request, I said I'd show you everything and just because I was good in that moment doesn't mean I hadn't been fucked up in the past—six times.

And you were silent. You were scared. You can't trust me. You wish you wouldn't have found out.

Now I'm still on the table and you're pulling every trigger. Everything I told you, you're doing right now. And remember that I didn't volunteer the information. It was requested, so doled out.

I want to be open. I want to be vulnerable. I want to be everything you deserve. Just please remember, too—No....

I'm actually over this whole thing. An incredibly fun fact: life is painful, so no shit love is going to be excruciating at times because it's the pinnacle of life.

I have nothing else to say at the moment.

If you'll allow yourself to forgive the loftiness of his seafaring style, you'll be able to cut to the core of the mad man keeping this log and see that he is desperate to be in love to the point of delusion. But when the smallest obstacle or the slightest hint of rejection presents itself he is quick to cut the line and drift into oblivion on a life raft only big enough for one.

The offense which he alludes to vaguely in this final entry refers first to the woman in question inquiring about his previous relationship, to which he responded honestly and openly only to be met with disgust, criticism, and jealousy. Second, as her retort that is completely unmentioned in the entry itself, the woman had then set an ultimatum that is uniquely and horrifyingly Millennial: he must follow her on social media and like five of her posts.

It was this ultimatum that sent him reeling. Social media had long since been a stressor in his previous relationship, and so he pleaded with the girl, explaining to her that in doing so it would without a doubt spark a conversation between him and his ex that he was not ready to have. But she insisted vehemently, and eventually he caved.

In the morning he received a text from his ex. It was a screen grab from the social media app showing that he had started following Alice and liked five of her pictures consecutively—and nothing else.

His heart sped up and his breath became shallow as his anger grew. At the girl who set the ultimatum, at his ex who monitored him, at social media for a number of reasons, including prolonging heartbreak. At himself for giving in to all of it and being an active part of the problem. At himself for knowing his past would always haunt him. At himself for everything. And though he didn't realize it yet, "angry at himself for being angry at himself."

Later that afternoon, when he sat down to write the final entry, he made a cold decision regarding the way he would sign off. Although it was only two letters that were absent, the missing "xo" had considerable implications. It meant goodbye.

***

To date, one of his favorite Christmases had been spent in Portland, Oregon the year that his brother came to visit him. Christmas just the two of them in the rain, drinking beer with orange juice as they played pool, going to the movies, eating Chinese food, etc. Simple shit. Magical, festive.

Although special enough in its own right, the event that magnified this holiday was on Christmas Eve when the brothers were joined by a third party named Maggie.

She was his manager at the local gourmet sandwich shop and convenience store where he worked and she was originally from Portland so was naturally in town for the holidays. Following an afternoon of pool and beer OJ's, and given the rain and all, it seemed appropriate that she would invite them to her parents' home for dinner that evening. Without a call to her folks or any fair warning, the brothers accepted and off the three of them went.

The house was on a tree lined street in an affluent neighborhood in NE Portland and appeared to be something out of a painting. Not in a lazy way either. Sitting safely behind a cobblestone wall, the way the warm light from indoors reflected off the wet grass in the lawn reminded him of something he had literally seen in a painting. He recalled seeing it and imagining the life within it as one he would strive for.

Once inside, he discovered that his vision was surprisingly accurate and the American idyll was alive and well and attainable. They were greeted by the smell of baking bread, a wall of warmth, and an even warmer hug from Maggie's mom in the kitchen. With a shake of her dad's hand and one from her brother who was in town visiting from college, they were at once a part of the family.

He made himself at home, washing his hands and helping Maggie's mom prepare the Cornish hens with butter, garlic, and rosemary while drinking red wine. After popping them in the oven there were 45 minutes of waiting in pure bliss, left hovering in that perfect moment right before anticipation meets actualization. The epitome of the holiday itself. This was Christmas. And a very fucking merry one at that.

All this to elucidate the special bond that he had formed with Maggie, and the backbone which formed his idea of a perfect future with her. It was that night he thought of when he learned she would be coming to Los Angeles for a week of job interviews in preparation for a potential move. It was that night he thought of when he offered to let her stay at his place for the week.

They had maintained a casual, distant friendship over the years. One that since his first year in LA almost eight years ago had dwindled pretty much just to an annual Merry Christmas text or email, but had recently formed into a more intimate, though still distant one that involved regular FaceTimes about life, relationships, and aspirations. There was a closeness between them that allowed for no personal detail to go unmentioned, as they were very similar in nature and in reality had known each other, or at least known of each other, for going on 10 years.

Being that the quickest way to crush an illusion is to live with it, it's no surprise that shit went awry fast. What began as an excited visit morphed almost instantly into a floundering relationship that would never work out. Her therapist had warned her to not get drunk with him, and certainly not to sleep with him. But therapists are paid to listen, not necessarily be listened to—right? Within a day—*24 little hours*—they had their first argument, which he remembered only vaguely in the morning and her not at all due to excessive drinking. And though the exact details of the argument remained a mystery, there was still an unspoken understanding that something dark existed there, and the pressure to overcome it was insurmountable.

For the next week they tiptoed around each other in a cordial and heartbreaking attempt at making the best of her visit. But neither was a trained dancer so one was bound to stumble at some point, especially considering the drinking. And they did stumble, grabbing each other as they fell on her last night in town.

They had gone to dinner at a fancy restaurant that night and were drunk by the time they got home in spite of all the bone marrow toast and duck ragu gnocchi. It was late and they laid on top of the sheets in all their clothes with a fresh bottle of wine as she broke it down for him clearly. There was no future for them. They were too similar and lost in their hopeless discontent, with all of the other usual symptoms that accompany unrealistic expectations. It was true, but awful to hear. Once put into such plain terms it could no longer be ignored, the illusion shattered. They became sullen and quiet until finally she fell asleep. His eyes were still open. There was still wine in the bottle. His heart twisted and wrung out with such an obvious truth. So then, what was the point?

He hung onto this question as he sat up on the edge of the bed and took a small swig from the bottle. His phone was nearby. He checked the time: 1am. He set it down. Then picked it up again and texted: "Just finished dinner. You still up?"

Dani: "Yeah. Come over." Then: "Bring rosé."

With sad determination he stood and took a deep breath. An almost caricature-like expression of himself, and his disappointment and loneliness. Just a big dumb fuck leaving his own home in the middle of the night, never to see the sleeping girl again.

She was from Singapore by way of Australia and it had a lasting impression on her accent. Americans are idiots about accents, and this particular American was no exception. He heard it for the first time over the phone when Dani called him one day at work and it came as a surprise. It all came as a surprise. Everything always seemed to come as a surprise.

They started seeing each other in the weeks before Maggie's visit. Having met through an app and talked a few times over the phone, they finally met late one night after many previous failed attempts when Dani was on her way home and chose to take a U-turn to head to his place in Koreatown instead.

When she arrived it was just to talk. And they did for hours. About what it doesn't matter at this point, only that it was easy and natural. She was deeply understanding, intuitive, and generally a badass. Sensitive yet tough, a cancer survivor with a unique perspective on love and a beautiful voice. Not just because of the accent. In fact, the accent disappeared when she sang. It was more her tough sensitivity and that unique perspective on love that lent itself so well to her voice and the words that beautiful voice was singing. She even won best young songwriter of the year back where she's from. *Generally a badass.*

She would later write a song about that first night they met and send him an early demo via text. This was after things quickly went south, when both learned that they could match each other's messes and although her perspective on love has been said to be unique it also happened to be uniquely shared by the two of them.

In fact, this was generally the case when it came down to it. If you could get rid of all the superficial and antiquated shit surrounding sex, love, and relationships, it was not an issue of gender. Speaking strictly in the context of consensual dating on level playing fields of power, of course. In the dating world, the issue was generational. Everyone was seeing everyone because they were all available—everywhere—and all looking for The One in the vast web that encompassed the world. Like the story about the camel in the desert, stuck halfway between two Oases and unable to make a decision between which one to drink from so ultimately drops dead. Only this one is on crack, because it involves humans and it's about love and the decision isn't just between this oasis or that one, it's a decision that must be regarded in the scope of All Oases across the whole world. Everyone's fucking dying. Quite literally yes, but emotionally too.

Although things went south with Dani, deep south all the way into hell, when they arrived there they found they had a friend in each other. He had eventually found a friend in Lara too. And once you came to this realization you were free. You were no longer in hell, you were simply at the bottom with nowhere to go but up from there and some good folks around who would help you climb out.

It's fantastically liberating, this notion of platonic love. And an easy one to overlook while in the midst of the devastating journey of seeking out that grand idea of The One. But if you enter into these things openly and honestly, if you make yourself vulnerable to the infinite possibilities that mutual respect allows, the rewards are invaluable. Everyone is teaching or learning something from each other, even if it's for the second time. Everyone will be OK.

He had perhaps known this already as a younger man, but grown callous as time went on and ultimately selfish. Everyone had their own story and each must be listened to and regarded with the sanctity you would your own. While on that subject, it is important to point out here that he has previously made casual mention of certain friends and love interests in a way that they appear as peripheral snapshots within a certain text. This is not due to some deluded narcissism, but due to the aforementioned mutual respect he has for them and a deep and genuine love. He had learned the lesson much earlier in his life that sometimes it is best to let folks tell their own story. Especially when you respect and genuinely love them, because although you might have the best of comical intentions in mind and be open to all kinds of self-deprecation yourself, others might simply enjoy their privacy. And if they don't, they're certainly capable of framing their own experiences and exposing them in whatever manner they so please.

To those who do appear somewhere within said *certain text*—namely, right here in this absurd Self-Help farce—it is only inasmuch as your tangential experiences need to be expressed in relation to his own. With respect. And love. And with the sincerest of gratitude, because without you he would likely not still be alive, and even if he were it would likely not be a life worth living. Because of you—because of everyone—all is possible.

With that, it is certainly time for a shot of rosé. Please cue: *"True love will find you in the end."* The original by

Daniel Johnston. Both very good for the heart, and for your health.

XI

AFTER A DEEP AND HOPEFUL SLIDE into her DMs with an aggressive proposition to meet specifically on Monday or Tuesday—the two days where bar patrons primarily consisted of alcoholics and were typically considered "weekend recovery days" by the rest—he immediately ghosted due to unforeseen events involving super fries, tears, family, and work. Events unrelated.

It dawned on him several days later that they hadn't spoken since, and in the clarity of his sobering 2.30am post-bar meal, he pulled out his phone and dictated a message. A message he can no longer remember, but must have been equally profound as it was captivating. Something like: "Hey." Then waited with bated breath for a response.

When the response came the following day at a far more respectful hour it was with wry simplicity: "Way to slide in and then slide the fuck back out."

She couldn't resist giving him a hard time under the circumstances, which he welcomed gladly with self-deprecating obligation. And although giving him a hard time, she did it in a way that expressed humor, patience, and understanding. All this before they even met, which he not only appreciated but actually needed terribly.

It was agreed they would meet that Saturday at a bar called The Three Clubs. He got off work at 5pm on Saturdays and was typically two drinks deep by 5.30pm, so it was decided they would meet as close to that time as possible. Having already made a great first impression before their first in-person encounter, it seemed only natural that he would take things further by arriving 25 minutes late to meet her.

Micki: French or Latin or Hebrew in origin, meaning close to God, or who is like God. A gift from God. And that she was. She entered his life with such perfect cosmic timing that it was impossible to refuse. Not that he would have anyways.

Standing at 5-foot 4-inches, she was decidedly of Polish descent with magnificent overly large blue eyes that at once demanded one's attention. The type of eyes that could be felt across the room if they even so happened to glance at you, which proved to be even more powerful given her habit of staring. Later, at the only dive bar that existed in Carmel, CA while on a very short and romantic getaway, he recalled having to peel her gaze away from a group of locals that had attracted her attention by performing what seemed to be a sort of melodramatic dinner play put on out of some upper class small town boredom, but turned out to be a very real interaction as a result of said upper class small town boredom. She took an interest in life, and in people, which was less scientific in its fascination than it was pure amusement and childish joy in how bizarre this life was as well as the people that inhabited it. He liked that about her.

It was those eyes that he first noticed about her, followed quickly by her sharp wit and candid, cutting sense of humor. She was really fucking funny. Saying nothing of her physical beauty at the moment, which he was certainly enamored with. But as they entered the bar on that first evening it was the way she made him laugh that attracted him most. Between catching his breath he found himself wondering when it was he had forgotten how to laugh—at least like this. A laugh that was not burdened by some underlying obligation or joined with equal parts sadness, but was honest and simple. It was her sense of humor that would become the foundation on which his love grew, like a laugh itself, starting deep within the gut and trailing upwards through the heart and out of the mouth and eyes, setting off a tidal wave of endorphins in the brain and in the body as a whole.

That night he laughed a lot. So much that his stomach felt taut in spite of all the booze he consumed, and crow's feet seemed to materialize at the corner of his tearing eyes. Was she the funniest person he'd ever met? There were so many funny people in the world, she countered, at which he thought, 'So many funny people, indeed. But humor is subjective and taking into account all aspects of your humor and person, your brand of funny brings me the most joy.'

He thought further, 'A lot of people can tell a joke, but few can make their audience, however small, fall in love over a laugh.'

As he relished over this thought he realized that it wasn't just laughing like this that he had forgotten how to do, it was this manner of thinking as well. Short and plain thoughts that were almost philosophical in nature, but more so just peaceful, contemplative, and introspective. For so long he had been spiraling in a dark web of self-destruction that at some point his once jovial de-meanor became sullen and he found himself taking all of this far too seriously. It was as if she were bringing him back to life, guiding him like a bright light that stretched and bent, reaching inside the tunnels of his bullshit and illuminating the darkness to bring him back to the sur-face. He remembered now that this life of heartbreak might be just one cosmic joke. And he laughed again.

With that in consideration he could breathe again. He had caught his breath. Like an antivirus carried by the digital four winds, she was caught in his lungs and ran rampant through his bloodstream henceforth, ravaging his foolish, self-imposed isolation from the inside out and recalibrating his hard drive completely. As if that were a thing.

***

Always cool, calm, and collected on the surface, if you looked at her closely you could see that the stress actually manifested itself in tiny, ever persistent strokes—baby strokes if you will—that were especially evident when she went to ash her cigarette. When she wasn't smoking they were basically invisible. A constant though imperceptible shudder through her body. But he didn't know her when she didn't smoke. He realized he might not even know her at all. And that terrified him because if he didn't know her, how could he already feel what he did? Was she even real?

He had come across her profile on a dating app, but she didn't respond. The account was inactive. That's when he slid into her DMs.

"I'm not real," she told him. "Major stroke got me a few years back. When I said I was ghosting around *Ramble*, I meant life."

They had known each other for approximately a month, and much of that had been spent with the entire country between them due to her rigorous work schedule of two weeks on, two weeks off. How much of this had been made up? Was he going crazy again? An impossible question to answer, but to insert a small yet significant detail that may touch on the matter somehow and in some way: it was October and he was listening to Christmas music. Worse, it only made him want to be with her more.

It was her work that caused the stress, mainly, and it was her work that made it so that he couldn't be with her at that particular moment. She was in Florida maybe, or Maine. Either way she was gone.

He missed her. The way she slept in through his first two alarms in the morning, then would always wake up on the last. With one eye open she would inevitably roll over and wish him a good morning, kissing him gently before falling back asleep. He missed the way her hair would sometimes fall to one side of her head in an absurd moment that made it look like a toupee, and the way her eyes would roll up into their sockets jokingly as she shook her head to move her hair back into position. The way she would give him shit with a smile as her lower jaw poked out in a mischievous under-bite before prodding him lovingly in the ribs. The way she would finish her food first, without fail. The way she would make sure they were always touching when they slept, even if two feet were between them—just an errant toe touching his.

The way she would laugh and tell him to "look away, Sir!" anytime she was embarrassed. The smell of her fresh face after she washed it at night. The feel of her soft skin caressing his. Her long nails running along his arm or back. Her dry and earnest tone that could fool a lesser trained listener into thinking she was serious when it only incited him to laughter. Her face. Her smile. Her lips. He really fucking missed her.

It was her work that had taken her away. She didn't smoke when she was at work, and how could he know her then? She was so far away. They spent half their lives apart from each other. A life spent in segments, two weeks apart and then two together. It was a devastating schedule, but one he endured due to the value in which their time together held for him. What was the alternative anyway? To give her up altogether just because he couldn't always have her all to himself? He was absolutely an idiot, but there was hope for him yet. She gave him that hope.

Her work he didn't dare mention, as it involved a celebrity couple. Delicate enough as is, yet more delicate still when you knew that the celebrity couple belonged to a certain religious organization that prided itself in its privacy. Not something he cared to disrupt. She was also a member of the organization itself, which he thought about no further than a fleeting, passive 'if it helps you and it doesn't hurt others then who cares.'

Look away then, sir. Look away from all that and right into her eyes. Pupils unbelievably dilated at all times as if she had spent too much time underneath the ocean. She had seen another world. She knew something he didn't. If nothing else, what she knew was how to be alone. And without realizing it, she was imparting this knowledge upon him.

It had become a well-rehearsed routine. A lesson plan taught without second thought. Teaching him how to be alone. He would watch her early in the morning every two weeks as she prepared to leave for the airport. It was a quiet affair, those last moments in the cool blue light of morning as he watched her finish packing. So quiet in fact that you could most certainly hear the sound of his heart breaking. He remained in the tangled sheets, cataloguing those final moments of her with meticulous sentimentality. A single tear dropped from his eye and rolled down his cheek. He knew that she was aware that he was awake, but he hoped she didn't notice the tear. As much as he would miss her, he didn't want the gravity of his longing to affect her in the slightest. This was the reality of her schedule and her work, and there was nothing he could do to change it. She had been very upfront about it, having very likely been through a number of short relationships that ended as a result of this very painful schedule. He refused to be a continuation of this cycle. He would cherish her presence and endure her absence. He would make it work.

Her steps were loud in the hallway as she left. And fast. They were always fast. She seemed to walk almost 2mph quicker than the average person, and for no apparent reason other than she had an innate sense of urgency about life. Each day was a list of have-to's and want-to's, objectives that she would complete with military precision. She was generally skilled and highly efficient. Being a task-oriented man himself, he admired these traits greatly. Just another thing about her that made his heart swell.

All of this he considered while still in bed as he listened to those fast footsteps get further away in the hallway then disappear altogether. She was leaving again. He hated when she left, but with these oddly clinical yet sweet thoughts of her, and with her smell still on the pillow, he smiled. An unusual sensation, to smile so early in the morning. More unusual still that the smile should be one experienced on his lonesome. She had given him all the necessary data and he was analyzing it in order to learn how to actually be alone. Which, like everything about her, *he not only appreciated but needed terribly.*

It was an invaluable lesson that he absorbed through his pores. For all of the love he had to give, he also wanted to get it back. When it wasn't reciprocated in the past it hurt like hell and he searched for it wherever it might be found. It still hurt like hell, but now he knew to look only inward, and find that love first for himself. That was the secret to truly being alone. And once you learned how to do that, only then could you know how to be with someone else. It would take time, but he eventually learned how to be alone. And then, too, he still knew he wanted to be with her. But, after all that, one day he opened his eyes and she was really gone—for good....

XII

WHAT THE FUCK HAS HE BEEN SAYING about me? I imagine it hasn't been good, and I'm afraid it's all been true. I overheard a detail here and there and although he kindly, and mindfully, neglected to use names, I am positively, certainly embarrassed that the "He" in the stories related were in reference to myself.

I'd have jumped in to defend my reputation had I not been overcome with sickness. What, with the flu going around and all. And then the holidays. Et cetera. And besides all that I wouldn't want my ego to come between you, the reader, and a solid piece of investigative journalism. Even(or especially) if I should be the topic of investigation, including all my flaws, as relatable as they may be.

In any case, I'm not the only one that has fallen ill in these past few months. My neighbor is dying. Between precisely 9 and 9.10am every morning I can hear him through the bathroom walls. It begins with a horrible gagging sound, then escalates into a hacking that is followed by projectile vomiting. You can tell it's projectile by the force with which it hits the toilet water. An awful and unforgettable noise. For 10 fucking minutes. Cancer maybe. Or sustained, long term alcoholism. Either way, it isn't good. He's on his way out.

In a twisted Borgesian fantasy/nightmare I have come to believe that the man dying on the other side of the wall is actually me. In a parallel or tangential universe that co-exists with this one in some bizarre shift in time, it's me dying in there after a series of decisions or nondecisions led me to become permanently stuck in this place. All the more reason for me to finally get the fuck out of here, because even if that isn't some bizarro version of me dying through the walls the fact that I can even think that for a second means there is something terribly wrong going on.

This place itself should be called attention to, which was perhaps most appropriately discussed in a letter that I recently sent to my manager by certified mail:

Dear [Manager],
This past year has been a tumultuous one: globally, politically, personally, professionally, etc. Historically so even, unfortunately. I know you've experienced your own difficulties, to say the least, to which I can do nothing but send my love and let you know that I'm here if you need anything.

As I'm sure you noticed in reading the first chapters of my new book, I've been a disaster. Between personal and financial issues, working 55 hour weeks at Galerie, trying to finish the movie, and delving back into prose in an attempt to write the new book, I've been more than overwhelmed. It probably doesn't help that I've continued to live in the same apartment which served as a "kill room" in Folie, Adieu where my character was essentially waiting to die. It may sound dramatic, but I do believe that it has had some very real psychological effects.

I'm sure you've had your own frustrations with me, as when I signed with you on April 13th of last year we were both under the impression that the movie would soon be done and we would find distribution before the holidays. The movie has suffered countless setbacks that have been infuriating and exhausting and there is yet an end in sight as we continue to struggle with post sound as well as music licensing. The book is deeply personal and a brutal endeavor no matter how much humor I approach it with. And I'm still scraping by to pay rent at that same damn apartment.

With April 13th now approaching again not far in the distance I wanted to officially give 30 day notice that I would like for our contract to not be renewed. Having not gained the momentum with the movie or otherwise that we both anticipated, it doesn't seem fair that either of us should have any contractual obligations to each other. Letting myself down is one thing, but having the burden of letting someone else down is too much bear.

Please don't take this personally or as a termination of friendship. Moving forward I not only hope to maintain our friendship, but also a business relationship that might be considered an open one. I can't say enough how grateful I am for your encouragement and insight, for your constructive criticism and feedback, and for your guidance in general. I can't thank you enough for having faith in me and in my work. Even that alone has been invaluable. The formality of this whole thing seems strange, but it's what the contract requires, and I know you'll not only understand my position but will most likely agree that this decision is for the best for the both of us. With all this considered, I still remain optimistic about the future—out of necessity. If I didn't believe it were going to be bright as fuck I'm not sure this darkness would be bearable. And I hope to see you when I get there.

With gratitude and so much love.

Of course, that's not verbatim, but it gets the general idea across. My Executive Producer Noelle wouldn't dare let me send a letter as flowery and sentimental as that. When she read the first draft she laughed at me over the phone, saying, "Elijah, you cannot send a letter like that! You have to cut it down and get straight to the point! Don't be so emotional."

After trying to explain to her that without my sensitivity and genuine fondness of other human beings I might simply be a piece of shit she still insisted I edit the letter down, which was definitely the right call.

Noelle is an amazing woman, inside and out. Remarkable in every aspect. By way of her lawyer, she had gotten my name awhile back when she was looking for a writer to adapt her book for the screen. The book was a fascinating historical fiction piece that paralleled a modern day story to that of Austrian Princess Leopoldina, who was married to the crown prince of Portugal and who ultimately helped declare Brazil's independence before her husband murdered her. Like the first Empress of Brazil herself, Noelle is both gentle and strong and doesn't have time for bullshit. She had me meet her an hour after our first phone call, telling me she'd be at a mall in Century City and that I would recognize her as "the tall blonde." Which I did, aided by her overtly European demeanor within a very American environment. There she was, a tall blonde with blue eyes, impeccable dress, and infectious enthusiasm. A multilingual German somewhere in her early and ageless 50's operating out of Berlin, Santa Monica, and Shanghai. A musician, a painter, a writer, a theatre director whose shows have been put on in Havana and in Vegas, and in general an old school badass.

A few days after the first meeting she gave me her book to see if I wanted to take on the adaptation. Upon her insistence, in person in the lobby at the Chateau Marmont over tea, she physically handed me the manuscript because she didn't trust sending it in an email. As I mentioned before: amazing.

This may seem like an aside, but it is important in that this amazing woman has since day one supported, trusted, and believed in me. And my manager stood up this amazing woman on three separate occasions they had arranged to meet. I learned this detail while Noelle and I were at our monthly white wine spritzer lunch in Beverly Hills. We always go to the same place and order the same Caprese salad and have a single spritzer each. And she always pays, agreeing that some day when I "make it" she will never have to pay again. On this particular day Noelle has brought me a check which accounts for half of the finishing funds for the movie and is accompanied by beautiful commentary in the vein of, "Elijah, what is this life of yours? You come to a free lunch and get handed a check? I want this life!"

I promise her that for as good as those two details sound in the same sentence, she does not want this life. To which she responds with the story about my manager standing her up on those three separate occasions and how I need to let her go. Which might be considered an odd jump in conversation, but it is really a natural progression when you're fitting a whole month into a single spritzer lunch and is something I had previously been considering anyway. Besides, *what if* Netflix is on the line? They want to buy the movie, but they can't get a response from my manager. *Disastrous implications.* Noelle is right.

Another good call, as hard as it was to follow through with the break up letter. If only Noelle were to have the final say in all of my life's decisions. For instance, when I was accosted by a do-gooder on the street and convinced to sponsor that little Filipino girl? She certainly would have advised against it. For me it took three months to realize I wasn't the right person for the job, and only when the automatic payment came out of my checking and overdrafted the account. Not that my heart wasn't in the right place, which is typically the case—but still….

A fine example of what has proved to be an overwhelming theme elsewhere throughout my life in general. In the desire to love and be loved I have made compromises to a fault. When not met in the middle, I have only compromised and extended myself further to the point of eventual resentment. It is within that resentment, however deeply buried in the subconscious, that the darkest mistakes have been made. For those mistakes I am sorry, but to finally understand their sad, underlying motivations is to realize that change is possible. It actually might even be easy. A simple acknowledgement that you will never have to settle and are deserving of love, and a decision not to overcompensate when that love isn't reciprocated, but instead just walk away because *you are deserving of love.* And walk away quickly, because it only gets harder with time.

They say "you should never have to apologize for the way you need to be loved." I'm not exactly sure who *they* are, but they're right. Never again. There is a way to make healthy compromises without sacrificing your integrity—in romance, in friendship, and in business—that if properly and deliberately tended to from the start will at the very least minimize the pain either party will experience should the bond be broken, and at the most will forge something beautiful and lasting. It's balance. It's symbiosis. Not weird or rocket science.

This is not to place blame elsewhere for any of my previous actions, rather it's the opposite. We have an obligation to ourselves to understand our patterns and needs, and move forward in our interactions accordingly. And it's certainly not to justify any of my previous actions either, which would be an impossible act and a deplorable one even to attempt. But it is to make sense of them. There is reason to everything. When the wife murders her cheating husband it's not justified, but at least it makes sense. Just like when your manager stops showing up or responding to your calls you leave them, or when a little Filipino girl needs money you send it to her. If it all didn't somehow make sense then it would just be pure madness.

Concerning my notable absence in X and XI, they need not be justified either, though I would like to offer an explanation given the respect I have for our friendship and this ongoing transparency. For starters, in spite of the bleak mention of the status of the movie in the letter, it is finally done. After shooting it in just eight days in December of 2016, then taking one day off, we turned around the first rough cut in just seven days, finishing at 4pm on my 30th birthday. I recall taking a shower—in this very apartment which I currently write, where the movie itself was written too, as well as shot, edited, and reviewed ad nauseam—and feeling a sense of relief that my 20's had come to a close. All of the hard work I had put in could finally begin to pay off.

Now one year and three months later I sit here on March of 2018 as a 31 year old man with a finished movie that the world has yet to hear of. Having done a private screening last April to positive reviews, we still spent the time between then and now in post-production sound hell. The last four months have been specifically horrendous, as in early November we were struck with a blow concerning music licensing rights and had to switch out over half the music in the film while shuffling around the other songs that had already been pre-cleared. This required cutting in countless other test songs while on the fly, exporting them from a laptop and uploading to my producer/editor Joel(god bless you for everything), my producer Liam in New York, my music supervisor, and Noelle—all while at work at Galerie.

At some point Galerie moved me away from the labor and into the office, which came with a small raise and a significant amount of added responsibility. I am no longer a blue collar worker at a white collar job, I am a shop boy whom the clients go to for pricing/info/invoicing/etc. All day I walk them back and forth from our main space to our two warehouse spaces down the street, traversing the alley between other calls and emails. A myriad of emails have been sent in regards to every single item in our collective 10,000+ square feet of space. I knew nothing about furniture when I helped unload that container five years ago. Now I can recognize the difference between an early or later production of a Jeanneret piece, I know Prouve, Perriand, Nakashima,

Royere, Mogensen, Mollino, Zanuso, Johansson-Pape, Tynell, Henningsen, Chapo, et al. The ceramics too: Axel Salto, Arne Bang, Stig Lindberg, Berndt Frieberg, Carl Harry Stalhane, Gunnar Nylund, and so on. I can tell you that the dining table is $120K, the chair is $74K, the easy chair is $14K, the stool is $5,800, the lamp $4,200—what the fuck. Not only that, but I can recall to whom I've sent the details to in an email in the past so that when a client asks I know specifically where to search in the sent mail to find the proper images/info/pricing/dimensions. There are two lines between each photo in the emails pertaining to the same item and four lines that separate the different items. Everything is a formula. An insane formula in high volumes that make massive profits—for the partners.

I have begun to dream in emails. Starting around 5am I wake up sweating under the pressure of knowing that a certain client is expecting certain information and they need it immediately. For the next four hours it is my pleasure to be in a partial dream state, drafting this imaginary email to this imaginary client with pricing and information on the bed I'm sleeping in, the nightstand and dresser, the lamp, and anything else in the very room I am in. I can feel my eyes scanning through the emails on the back of my eyelids as I scroll through the various photos in search of the right pieces.

The alley, too, has crept into these dreams. It flashes in sporadically, cutting between the emails for a moment here and there with its sights and smells. The oily puddles and onion skins behind the Indian restaurant. The occasional scent of hot dogs wafting down from the famous joint on the corner. The stagnant water left in the vases at the floral shop. The chemicals and spray from the paint at the auto body shop. The dirty, swollen feet of the transients and their almost perpetually exposed ass cracks. Not your garden variety homeless either. This particular stretch of Melrose is still affected by the heavy gang activity of its past and still makes a killing off drug sales, as well as it suffers from the new influx of homeless that got pushed out of Santa Monica. They have nowhere else to go. The alley is their bedroom, their party house, and their bathroom. It pains me to say that somewhere within this mess my ability to identify the pieces within this world extended itself into the alley as well. It's easy to tell the difference between a dog's shit and a human's, but when you're able to guess confidently at that human's age, height, weight, gender, and race you've got a real problem.

"Always be better than the job, but never too good to do the work." I've repeated those words to myself for as long as I can remember. So long that I actually can't remember if I said them first myself, or had heard them elsewhere. It's been an important mantra that has stuck with me through every odd job imaginable as I quietly write my books or scripts at night or early in the morning, living an ambitious fantasy while accomplishing the tasks at hand.

I remember the day The New York Times review of "Mother Fucker" came out, mentioning my name and calling it a *smart, understated sex comedy*. Trash was strewn around the Galerie parking lot and a used condom was leaking its contents onto the pavement. I put on rubber gloves and took care of it all, letting the lid to the dumpster slam shut after the trash bag was safely inside, sure to not rip or tear the bag for fear of *its contents leaking out*. What is *The New York Times* anyway?

There was a time when I looked forward to dreaming, even dedicating a certain period of the day to dreaming itself as I researched the somewhat elusive qualities of lucid dreaming in my late teens. My dreams were filled with flying and fucking and success and travel and love and family—*my* family even, including wife and children. That was a long time ago, but even then they would sometimes come with their own darkness: teeth falling out, mangled limbs, cars crashing into the ocean, sharp objects being driven through organs, paralysis. Stuck there, immobilized by this self-induced dream, a presence would sometimes walk into the room. They would slowly come to the bed and stand over me, then gently put their hand around my neck before squeezing tightly. But without fail, I always woke up.

The rats came in the other night, here *in the same apartment which served as a "kill room" in Folie, Adieu where my character was essentially waiting to die*. It started with the clacking of their claws on the wood floors as I was half asleep in a fever dream. I thought it was my dog Gwenny at first, and that brief moment of overwhelming joy was followed quickly by the crushing and terrifying fact that it was not her at all, but a whole family of rats. They enclosed quickly upon the bed and scurried up the sheets to my horror.

Of course they weren't really there. When I woke up there was no one there. I was all alone here in my apartment in Koreatown much like I am right now. It's just like my buddy Joel said, "Just 'cause you can see your demons doesn't make 'em any friendlier."

It is this point that brings me back to the letter to my manager, which I only related earlier in order to illustrate this sea change I am currently undergoing, and perhaps soften the blow of the following letter, which I'm sure you've been expecting, even if not by certified mail:

Dear Reader,

With the utmost respect for you, and yet a deeper bond formed between us in our shared experiences of the mental and physical anguish caused by anxiety and other shit illuminated in the preceding pages, I, the writer, wish to say farewell.

It has recently come to my attention that as heartwarming and beneficial as this relationship has been, it's no longer working. It would seem that certain aspects of ourselves can sometimes not be overcome completely. They will be a part of us forever, and by identifying their causes and our reactions to those causes, we are able to better manage these afflictions even if we aren't able to get rid of them altogether.

Please don't take this goodbye personally or as a termination of our friendship, sweet lovers. It is simply a step forward, which is obviously a necessary step in the bigger picture of Moving On.

Henceforth, I hope that you will carry this with you like a picture of a loved one kept in the band of a helmet, or in a wallet, or on a cellphone background, because it's really fucking scary to go into this shit alone. However you do take it, please keep in mind that unsolicited advice is a favorite pastime of humans. Everyone claims to have their shit together. Everyone wants to tell you how to get your shit together. *I'm so fucking happy and here's how you can be happy too*:

Transcendental meditation will fix everything. Eat better and exercise. Make decisions for yourself. You need to just go out and have sex. Not gross sex either. Good sex with someone you're attracted to, but has no connection to your inner circle. Go back to your Ex. There's still so much love there. Don't go back to your Ex. Even if you miss her it's not right. Maybe you need to date someone else just to realize you actually want to be with your Ex. But will that still be an option if you date someone else? You realize it's just a dead end with your new girlfriend, right? Take better care of yourself. Get over yourself. You need to go to THERAPY. Seriously man, you gotta try transcendental meditation.

Some advice is better than others obviously. Some should be considered and heeded. Some is just common sense. Some should be ignored completely. But in general, if it's unsolicited then it's going to leave a bad taste in the mouth and the stomach probably won't digest it.

That being said, if this book has found its way into your hands and you've made it this far then perhaps none of this could be considered *unsolicited*. And though we haven't discovered a cure, I hope I haven't let you down. Letting myself down is one thing, but having the burden of letting you down is too much to bear.

If there's a moral to this letter, or even to this story at large, perhaps it could be gleamed in a single bit of advice: do not take any from me. But don't let that discourage you, because in all this time my brain has not fully turned upon itself. The anxiety and other shit has yet to kill me. Let that stand as a beacon of hope. We have a fighting chance. In all this time, I've managed to stay alive.

That fact alone—that we exist—is so fucking crazy. Let us never be so casual about it. No matter what you believe about *how* you got here, the fact that you can no longer exist at any given moment is just as crazy. Even crazier most of the time, as no matter what you believe about *what* happens after you go, there's typically no way of saying *how* you'll go.

And what of your beliefs about what happens after you go anyway? Present me with some facts. Send word when you get there. I'm open to discussion. Better yet, don't. I'm terrified of ghosts. If you go—when you go—just keep your secrets to yourself. Don't you dare fucking haunt me. It would be deeply upsetting.

For all of life's mysteries, I am okay to live in its one certainty: Now. Which I fully intend to enjoy. And I hope you do the same.

With gratitude and so much love.

xo,
Elijah Mallick

AT THE BOTTOM
OF THE ORCHARD
An Illustrated Fable

LIFE

THE SKY IS LIT UP LIKE THE INSIDE OF A GLACIER —a cool phosphorescent blue that contains neither sun nor moon. The only disruption in its icy dusk is an occasional flock of birds—feathers of a near celestial white— flying in zig-zag patterns and alternating letters of the alphabet toward an unspecified location which, surely, could only be better than that which they have taken leave.

Floating indifferently through the migrating birds is a single red balloon. Being carried within it is a folded piece of paper bearing a handwritten note:

I directed them back
On The Good River Path
At Godspeed.

Three Hundred Feet Below, watching what is now a red prophetic dot in the mentholated sky, is The Author of this note. A man of indeterminate age—pushing thirty or forty maybe, or seventy—with close cropped, slightly tussled black hair, eyes like tarnished brass, and an angular, OK-looking face. Above his thin, partial smile The Man has a well-groomed mustache which he decidedly kept just moments ago while shaving at his outdoor sink. He thought it would be both humorous and disarming.

Positively correct in his assumption, the mustache suc-
ceeds in making The Man look like an actor who has
made a slight modification in his appearance to prepare
for his upcoming role in a comedy.

Very few attempts have been made at directly recre-
ating The Man's appearance, and each of those attempts
does him a great injustice. Regardless, I will provide one
here:

This unfortunate illustration aside, The Actor in this
comedy, and The Author, stands seemingly healthy—
lean, confident—in the rubbery green grass at the bottom
of an apple orchard. Above him the evenly spaced rows
of squatty, ground-hugging trees with flat blossoms the
color of the birds' feathers crosshatch the side of a steeply
graded hill in Immaculate Order. Within the trees, in different stages of formation, is the invaluable blood shade
of their fruit.

The placement of the trees on such a hill makes gathering the fruit a simple task, described as follows: once fully ripened, gravity pulls the apples heavily from their boughs down towards the earth wherein the almost synthetic grass absorbs the impact; gently, stem over butt, the apples then follow the downward course of the slope until reaching the very bottom where, stretched tightly between two posts set on opposite ends of the lower perimeter, a net like that of a fisherman's catches the apples and safely harnesses them. At this point they can be collected at will by Our Man.

It is said that this placement of the orchard itself was a very calculated and smart decision, being that it is situated on a plot of land that covers an ambiguous stretch of popular trade route somewhere between Paris and Sad Francisco, anywhere, in the wide open space of a vast countryside like that of a fairytale. It is also said to be a mystery how The Man procured the property, and for what length of time he kept it. No one ever ventured to ask so blatantly. For all we know he has been there forever and ever.

What we can confirm about The Man's incalculable residence on the orchard is that his only company has been provided by travelers of the popular trade route it borders. They are decent folks, mostly, who find it a convenient stop to barter, trade, and sometimes give away their goods or services. Though their arrivals are unpredictable, sporadic, they have allowed The Man a very simple and comfortable existence. It is surprising to learn how little is truly needed to live. It is equally surprising to find how easy it is to accumulate the unnecessary, the trivial. As a reminder of this, or perhaps just to amuse himself, in the pocket of The Man's charcoal grey slacks he carries a lemon colored bouncy ball. The ball was once given to him for the price of two apples and a glass of water, although it is a custom of his to dispense water freely.

Still concealed in his pocket, The Man holds the ball between his fore- and middle fingers as he loses sight of the heaven sent note from his vantage point at the bottom of the orchard. Below the prickly hairs of his fantastic mustache a smile trembles as if it were preceding either a laugh or a good cry. Doing neither of those things, The Man turns around with his smile fading and begins the short walk to his home.

Fifteen feet away in a small home that paradoxes a sort of modern, backwards Thoreau-type inhabitance—a single room furnished with writing desk, chair, mattress, trunk, icebox, and helium tank—The Man removes the lemon colored bouncy ball from his pocket and ricochets it from hand to floor to wall back to hand at his standpoint in the room's center.

An adult, or an intellectual, or really any sane person subjected to the learned habits of logic and skepticism, may wonder at the likelihood of The Man attaining a helium tank for his own personal and prolonged use. How did he come across such a ludicrous accessory? To digress, for the sake of guaranteeing a degree of authenticity with these inquisitive peoples—though The Man would, in fact, find this digression to be ludicrous—it should be said that he received it as a gift.

One day a traveling circus found themselves in need of water at the time they came upon The Man's humble dwelling. The Clown was chosen from their group to ask The Owner of the home if they might draw from his well to provide for themselves and their animals—it would be a long journey to their next stop.

Upon seeing our dear gentleman's way of living, the decor of the home mainly, The Clown forgot his request and immediately renounced his craft. Something about the bare walls brought The Clown to tears. Their forlorn purity, their naivety, he said, touched him deeply. As proof of his affinity for the decorator of those walls which had touched him so, having sworn off his profession already, The Clown left the quintessential helium tank along with a duffel bag stuffed full of yet-inflated red balloons to the disposal of his inspiration.

After retrieving water for the circus folk and their animals, which The Man had done intuitively in spite of the forgotten request, he was perplexed to find such gifts waiting at the feet of the sobbing clown. Nonetheless, without questioning the gesture, The Man accepted the gifts graciously and watched as The Clown vigorously washed the make-up from his face.

The Caricature Artist that ran with that particular circus at that particular time, having been very thirsty and finished his water in one swallow, had come to ask for a second glass of water so was nearby to witness the spectacle. He was compelled to quickly sketch the scene:

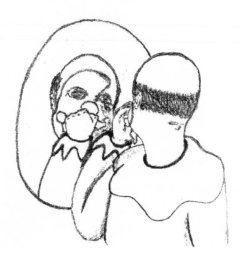

When The Artist handed the slip of paper with the sketch on it to The Man he was again pleased. He accepted the gift as graciously as the first, as he was never very picky about things so long as they came from the heart.

To put an end to this brief period of reminiscence, the glistening lemon-like sphere falls from The Man's hand to floor...bounce, bounce, bounce...to unmade bed sheets atop the mattress on the floor. In two strides The Man is at the bed and the ball is replaced in his pocket. With only vest and boots removed, he lies down flat on his back on top of the covers, switches off the lamp with a swift, absent motion of the arm, and stares in the ever-deepening blue of the dream filled night.

If this is not exactly how things were happening, it is at least how one man envisioned and recorded them, and how I will continue to give their account here.

* * *

IN THE SOFT, BLUE-GREEN CHALK PASTEL of the following morning, which looks just as any other morning on the orchard, The Man wakes up to tend to his daily rituals. First washing his face at the outdoor sink—and now trimming his mustache—then walking the length of the property along the catching net with a brown wicker basket to collect the ripe, fallen apples.

For reasons unknown there is a subtle disparity in the air this morning, similar to the muted excitement that precedes a departure. The Man, by way of his acute senses, is aware of something, but is unsure of exactly what. Casually, he eats the most perfect apple from the basket and continues about his morning as usual.

As custom permits, returning from his stroll The Man seats himself in the chair at his writing desk. From the duffel bag stowed away below the desk he extracts a limp red balloon. From the desk drawer he extracts a single, clean sheet of rectangular white paper and the black-inked pen he has used so often to commune with the heavens. Laying the sheet flat on the desk in front of him, he looks down at it to feel his mouth tremble with another of his unprovoked smiles.

'What of this joy of mine,' he thinks. 'It's going to be a great day.'

Just how great he is yet to discover, but in the hottest part of this day—his last on the orchard—when he prepares himself for a nap, his patience and diligence will finally come to a pinnacle. And he will be gone.

The Man's smile breaks into a loud, guttural laugh for reasons yet known to him, bending him over his desk until he exhales his laugh directly onto the page in front of him. Controlling the outburst, he sits up in his chair with smile still beaming beneath his mustache and he inspects the special stationery now containing his invisible laugh:

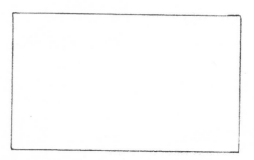

Meticulously, he then folds the paper in half six times along alternating vertical and horizontal axes like this:

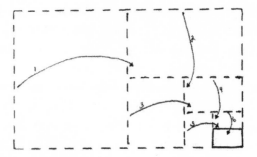

This now tiny piece of paper is then delicately inserted into the opening of the balloon, which he inflates at the helium tank then ties closed with a knot. To shake the balloon with the paper inside makes it rattle like a children's toy. The Man gently tugs the string he's attached to the balloon to produce that desired noise and effect a few times as he walks into his front lawn then comes to a stop.

Ceremoniously, this little custom of The Man's is concluded as he sets the balloon free and watches its leisurely ascent. There are no birds this morning to disrupt the balloon's flight, so it climbs steadily, casually, higher and higher, all the way up until it disappears into the still brightening sky.

* * *

IT DIDN'T IMMEDIATELY OCCUR TO THE MAN to employ the balloons in this manner. They underwent a variety of other uses first.

For awhile, The Man thought it might be fun to fill the balloons with water and hurl them at anyone whom he wished to be removed from his property. On a highly traveled path as such, and in so desirable a spot, it is inevitable you will encounter at least a few unsavory types. Only once, though, did he find the water grenade tactic suitable.

In a boxy, beat-up, rattling type of car, rusted most all the way through, came a middle-aged man driving with one hand while pressing the other to the roof of his car. If seen from close-up, The Driver had a greasy appearance, sweating, like that typical look of rundown men in bad movies and outside of city libraries. However, from far off The Man could only see the erratic clouds of dust caused by the car moving from pavement to gravel shoulder, back to pavement, back to gravel, growing nearer to the orchard.

The Driver was constantly checking the condition of his lap, glancing down at it then back up to the road. Each time he did this the car made one of its swerves onto the shoulder, then back off.

This strange manner in which the car was being driven alarmed The Man so much that he promptly filled a balloon at his sink and waited at the side of the road with it ready in hand. The car skidded to a stop.

"Hello, sir! Are you the owner of this orchard?" The Man confirmed to The Driver that he was the owner of the orchard. "I was hoping that you might be able to spare a few apples. Say two each for me and my girl?"

"Your girl?" The Driver looked into his lap again and whispered something. The head of the Driver's Girl popped into view. Her age was questionable and her vibrant red lipstick was smeared. The Man felt his intestines contract.

"She's a real beauty, right? This girl here is the most wonderful girl in the world." The Man contemptuously agreed with The Demon-Driver. "So, whaddaya say about them apples? My girl can make you a happy man."

"Well, I only have three apples on me," said The Man, for some reason showing the number on his middle to pinky fingers, which created a circle with his thumb and index as if to say O.K.

The Driver's Girl stretched her small arm out of the car window to where The Man was standing and poked her finger through the opening his hand gesture had created. Appalled, The Man quickly withdrew his hand, conscious of the weight of the water balloon in the other.

The Driver spoke again: "It must get pretty lonely out here all by yourself."

"A man always knows he's in good company when he's by himself," The Man replied. Not that he disliked the company of others—he was actually very fond of a great many people. But The Man also firmly believed that it was unnecessary to be dependent on the companionship of other humans in the world. There is enough solace to be found in nature, in the Self, in the Universe. "You can have these three apples," The Man told The Driver, "then I suggest you be on your way, please."

With that The Man handed The Driver the three apples he had been carrying in his pockets. The Driver returned a yellow grin. His Girl winked. A loud noise started from under the hood of the car, then the tires spun for a moment, gained traction, and The Driver and His Girl took back to the road from the shoulder with a second, equally horrible grating noise.

The Man was blinded by hot dust and burning rubber. Infuriated by the existence of this duo, and his powerlessness against them, he launched the water-filled balloon in what he thought was the direction the car had gone. It gave him no satisfaction. He shuddered.

* * *

THEN THERE WAS THE PARTY. No invitations were given out, but decorations were at least put up in preparation for one: several balloons bounced against the ceiling, one was tied to the knob on the front door, a few on the porch railings. Anyone who happened to arrive was welcome. And if no one came, The Man would still enjoy the festive look his home had undertaken.

Even a keg of fermented cider was rolled out that day from its storage beneath the house. The Man often poured himself a few glasses in evening hours as he sat down to whichever of the books he had procured from travelers. But this was a celebration—of sorts. He permitted himself to drink in abundance.

It had been a great length of time since he surpassed what he called his limit. The drink made him light at first. It gave him a sort of restless energy, like all things must be done at once. But what needed to be done? He drank more. His irritation and anxiety grew. His isolation intensified.

Drunkenness can have that effect sometimes on certain people. The brain swarms with ideas that will never be carried out and past actions that were carried out but not to one's satisfaction. It swarms with things that might solve all of one's problems and things that, in hindsight, most certainly would have solved all of one's problems but were abandoned before they could reach full potential.

The Man thought of all these things and considered his options. Solitude had, for the moment, lost its appeal. He had to get away. Genius struck him—or what he thought was genius at the time, in that state. He hurried about his home, rushing to build the contraption that would carry him away, like the birds, to somewhere that could only be better than where he was. He laughed, he cried, he tied, inflated, tied more, inflated, until the construction of his brilliant vehicle was finished.

In The Man's defense, the chair *was* equipped with enough balloons that it was able to hover—so long as no one sat in it. But with his added weight the device was a complete failure.

For the rest of the day and all through the night The Man sat outside his home in the failed contraption and imagined what it would have been like had he succeeded. He did not strain himself in taking into account all of the small things, such as the icy feel of the wind on his face at higher altitude, or the look of the countryside passing beneath him and the ease with which he might fall from his chair back into its green death below. He simply imagined floating, a lightness, the feeling of accomplishment, which all seemed like very nice things to him.

I could not find any actual sketches of what occurred in his imagination that day and night, but a very detailed description of the event was left behind and I have compiled those descriptions into my very own sketch of his mind's eye. This is what he saw:

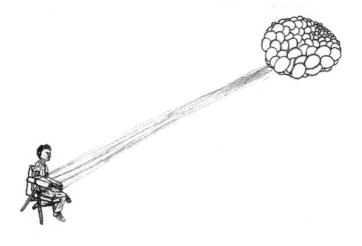

Of course, he did not have a mustache at the time, but for the purpose of continuity, and out of respect for the late Man, he will appear here in all but one drawing as he was last described to me. Besides, The Man himself never seemed to picture things the way they actually were.

By morning The Man had sobered up and felt very humbled. Almost excruciatingly so. He felt as if he had betrayed himself, his morals, his orchard. For the orchard his love and respect had been restored tenfold. For himself those things had been diminished. He felt no pity for himself though. Being an optimistic and resilient man, he told himself that it only meant he still had a long way to go. Piety, restraint, selflessness. That is what he strived for.

He considered it a blessing that no one had attended his party, therefore leaving him alone to experience his shortcomings in human behavior. He was very grateful for that smell blessing. It gave him the impression that someone was looking over him. And perhaps there was.

* * *

THE BALLOONS CONTINUED TO TORMENT The Man They sat in their duffel bag and he stared at them. He had always prided himself in his ability to find practical use for most of the things he acquired. As for those things for which a practical use could not be found, they were discarded unsentimentally.

The balloons were different. He knew they held some sort of importance. They must, because he could not bring himself to get rid of them. Of what importance they held he could not say. The answer evaded him. He re-

membered The Clown. He remembered the tears. He remembered a lot of things.

It occurred to him then to ask for advice. Even the
wisest of men can benefit from an outside source, even if
that source provides bad advice. From the most menial,
wrong, frivolous, and backwards things said it is possible
to extract great things, wonderful things. That is, if the
listener is truly listening. The Man resolved that he
would listen and set about asking the world for advice.
Starting with the birds.

They saw each other every day, The Man and the
birds, so he considered them the most logical acquaintance to approach. It would not be out of line to ask an
acquaintance a thing or two. He thought he would start
simply.

"Excuse me, little bird," he said to one of the migrating birds. "Where are you going?"

The Bird answered in a wonderfully feminine voice,
"On a-trip, a-trip!" It made The Man feel very happy.

"Where are you going on this trip?" asked The Man,
offering a handful of apple seeds to The Bird in his out-
stretched palm. The Bird, who was an extremely small
bird, perched on the very tip of The Man's finger and
took a seed in her beak.

Once she had swallowed the seed with some amount
of effort, she answered The Man for a second time, "On
a-trip, a-trip! I am going on a-trip, a-trip!"

The Man questioned patiently, though he was fairly
sure he knew what The Bird's answer would be at this
point: "But where does your trip end?"

"There is no end to the trip, a-trip!" said The Bird. "Everything is the trip, a-trip. But I must be going now. Thank you for the food for my trip, a-trip, a-trip!"

"...The Bird, who was an extremely small bird, perched on the very tip of The Man's finger and took a seed in her beak."

The Bird flew away to the nearest flock and joined their odd formation, though you could barely see its tiny wings flapping amongst the others'. The Man watched the birds and thought to himself, 'All their life they will fly back and forth, back and forth, without any real sense of direction and no expectations, and the Universe takes care of them.' He thought further, 'If only men could be more like the birds in their attitude towards life they would find themselves relieved of a great many burdens. Then again, we are not completely unlike the birds already....' As silly as it was, The Man chuckled at himself.

It was no longer possible to say which of the birds The Man had spoken with as the entire formation shrunk considerably into the distance. Still, he could remember the unique sounds of The Bird's voice and the memory itself was enough to make him happy. He didn't mind that he never got around to asking about the balloons.

* * *

THERE IS AN ETHEREAL QUALITY about waiting, about patience—the imperceptible stirring of celestial juices. Time continued to pass on the orchard in its usual, casual way. The ripened fruit fell from the trees and new fruit grew. Travelers came, traded, conversed, and carried on. The Man waited patiently for the solution to his balloon-riddle to come of its own accord.

Occasionally, The Man did make a half-hearted attempt at putting the balloons to use. But they were more for the sake of amusing himself. Once, he tied some of the balloons to a tree and they looked like giant, weightless apples. He liked that. More regularly though, it became The Man's practice to give out inflated balloons to the young travelers along the trade route as parting gifts.

In short, The Man lost no sleep over the balloons and the supply diminished only slightly as the great many balloons leftover slowly filled themselves with the light, careless breath of divinity.

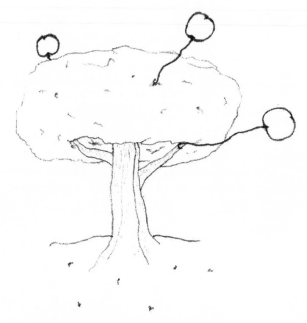

*"Once, he tied some balloons to a tree
and they looked like giant, weightless apples."*

On a cool afternoon, so clear under the azure skyscape, a little girl appeared on the orchard. She was a little thing, pale, alone, wearing a little peach colored dress with short, puffy sleeves. She couldn't have been more than eight years old and all by herself. The Man saw her coming down the road and wondered what someone so young was doing by themselves. Especially such a sweet little girl. He quickly arranged a gift: one balloon inflated to capacity(nearly ready to burst), a tall glass of water, and two carefully sliced apples with cheese. He even prepared a small bowl of oatmeal with chopped apples and a pinch of cinnamon and sugar. It was his intention to get her to stay for awhile until he could ensure she was safe. He was also very interested in hearing her story.

The strangeness of the girl's soft, silent steps approaching had an added gravity due to her soft, silent demeanor. Smiling, The Man called, "Hello!" from afar but nothing was called back. The Girl waited until she arrived to return the greeting, which still wasn't given in words, only a smile as tiny as her mouth and a slight nod of her infant-like head.

The Man continued to smile back and presented the gifts to her. The Girl tied her balloon to the front banister and took on her food and drink with an odd, almost disinterested gratification.

The way she consumed the food and drink was enough to prove her thanks if speech would not. It was certainly an extraordinary thing to watch her eat. The food and drink seemed to disappear without much effort. A few small, steady bites and the plate was cleared, the bowl was empty. The water was drained from the glass in one elegant sip. The Man was a bit startled by this, but delighted. She had given him a wonderful compliment by finishing his offerings, and now she eyed the balloon with the same odd look she had given the food.

"Would you like the balloon now?" It was clear The Girl would like the balloon now, but The Man posed the question anyway thinking that it might inspire a verbal answer. He stood with his back leaning against the porch railing and his hands clasped in front of him. He was excited to see what The Girl would do. The Girl said nothing to The Man, only burped slightly, covered her mouth with one hand, then shook her head resolutely in a sign that said, *of course* rather than a simple *yes*. The Man untied the balloon from the banister and handed it to The Girl.

With balloon in hand, The Girl smiled lovingly at The Man and took off towards the grass clearing directly in front of the house. The Man turned around from his position against the railing and leaned onto his elbows to watch. She was standing only fifteen feet away from him, staring at the gentle, stationary bob of the bright red balloon. The Man thought she looked quite peculiar, and old. The balloon, to him, looked quite peculiar as well, like a human heart beating on a tether. As he was thinking these things, The Girl raised the arm that held the balloon string between two fingers of its childish hand, and she let it go.

The girl's gaze was still held on the balloon, following the initial course of its ascent. The Man's gaze was cast likewise, but his perceptions were muddled by his previous thoughts. He watched The Girl freeing what was without a doubt a human heart.

The Man was astonished by what he saw, and by what he had neglected to see. As he watched the balloon-heart drift upwards into the sky, The Girl must have taken off in a mad sprint because when he shifted his focus back to her she was already on the top of the hill, standing on the road, waving goodbye.

* * *

THAT NIGHT THE MAN FELT UNSETTLED. Still, as he did not lose sleep over the balloons, neither did he lose sleep over the bizarre case of the little girl-woman, who was indeed the cause of his mood.

Had The Man taken to the common course of troubled men, who try to work out their issues within their own conscious reasoning, then everything quite possibly would have been different. However, with his sleep cycle unaffected, The Man slipped into unconsciousness that night and the dream took over.

The image of The Girl was so pervasive that it reappeared, naturally, in the forefront of the dream. As continuity need not be present in dreams, or an aesthetic concern while the sporadic images therein are spliced together, the image of The Girl came in all different angles and at varying distances. A close-up of her dress, her hand, the back of her head. A shot of her from the top of the hill, through the apple trees. Another close-up, from the perspective of the balloon heart: her extended arm and her tiny, pale face. With no explanation needed—again, this was a dream—this particular angle struck The Man personally. He was floating above The Girl. It was his heart she was holding. He was the heart and she was setting him free.

Slowly upwards. The Girl's features going out of focus, diminishing with the space covered. With the central point of The Girl's gaze becoming less distinct by sight, it was still clear to The Man that she was following his course, watching him. It was comforting to know that this little old soul was down there, somewhere, watching over him.

Rising further into the ether. Distinguishing lines that give shapes their recognizable forms, and names—nonexistent. Just a human heart floating calmly through an abstract colorscape. Thought still intact. 'So I am one of those people that dream in color,' thought The Dreaming Man. Communicative color nonetheless. Colors that speak in the no-tongue of basic principles. Pure gospel. 'Wonder if this is what artists try to recreate. Maybe some form of it, I suppose. I could not paint this, nor would I hang anything like it on my walls. But, oh my!'

For a moment The Man considered the words that made up his thoughts. Words did not matter. A wisp of white shot through the color. The words would get lost in the color, the wisp of white. They absolutely did not matter. 'Who am I? Where? What is this?' Those things did not matter either. Just the heart, the color, the light. He felt a slight shiver go through his body, half-paralyzed in bed.

Light flaring up around the edge of the dream. Like the orange flicker on a strip of film being projected on the eyelids. A spinning bed lamp showing fuzzy pictures of a sleepy childhood story. The orange flicker now creeping into the center of the dream, and the colors inching around the spectrum toward the halfway between true red and true yellow.

The true warmth of morning light shines through the blood vessels, at last taking over the entire frame. Coming back into the bright consciousness of after-dream. The bright light of a new morning. Awake.

* * *

THE MAN AWOKE THE FOLLOWING MORNING with his train of thought unbroken. It was as if his waking experience had not ceased during sleep, but shifted. Or, as he saw it, expanded.

'I was certainly there,' he thought to himself, putting on his grey woolen slacks and matching vest. 'A part of me was certainly there at least, and if that part can fully exist there, then I believe the whole can too.'

The Man was not unfamiliar with lucid dreaming, but this was the first time it had occurred in such logical forms. The dream had been free of clutter and of unnecessary or strictly amusing details. It seemed to consist of a simple idea and a simple feeling. Still thinking to himself, The Man asked, 'How to hold onto that feeling?'

He decided he would get the dream on paper. He had always been an avid record keeper and this was definitely worth noting. It meant something. In fact, most things in The Man's life he considered to *mean something*. His records cover a fantastic number of pages in small, neat print that if placed in one stack would be much taller than he. Without the existence of these notes, which I discovered in several hidden compartments about his abandoned home, these wonderful things would have gone unheard. It is from their vast, exceedingly detailed text that I report to you now.

If only his diligence, and maybe a little of our good fortune, would have extended into date-keeping. Then again, there is something special about being between places, where time is probably better measured in fragments of dream, fragments of hopes, excerpts from conversations, and three centered asterisks: where time is kept with the spirit, not the brain.

No matter the amount of meticulousness observed in record keeping of this nature, or the precise articulation of their author, there is an elemental loss when translating from spirit to heart to brain to paper. After the pen briefly hovered over the clean sheet of stationery, The Man made his first attempt at recording the dream:

I was there
In the dream—

Even with the vivid colors fresh in his mind, that was the poor start he made. He was dissatisfied by how obtuse it was of course. It would be better if he gave it away. And that act of giving!

The thing to do was obvious to him now, which was to simulate what The Girl had done. The Man then, for the first time, performed the actions that would become routine to him: he folded the slip of paper, inserted it into a limp balloon, inflated the blood-colored vessel from the holy tank, tied it, attached a string, and carried his messenger into the front lawn.

In almost the exact same spot The Girl had stood the day before, and again in his dream, The Man mimicked her maneuvers as best he could with one dignified arm held out and balloon string between his two fingers. As he let go of the little carrier pigeon he did not see a heart any longer. He saw a different sight: his head expanded and formed by latex, his face as pale pink as a swollen nipple on a hot day.

"He saw a different sight: his head expanded and formed by latex, his face as pale pink as a swollen nipple on a hot day."

Although it was equally strange as what he saw before, it did not make him run as The Girl had. Running was the only action of The Girl's which he thought unnecessary to perform. Instead, The Man sat down in the grass and reclined himself further yet onto the ground so that he was lying down.

Comfortably in repose, The Man shut his eyes, smiled, and gathered his thoughts into a pleasant, colorful nap.

* * *

OVER THE COURSE OF THE WEEK, after much consideration was put into the first exquisite dream and several short poems were sent out into the sky, The Man began to approach his naps methodically.

He undertook the naps as a sort of nontraditional scientific study of not just the dreams the naps harbored, but of the process of entering the dreams. Many different techniques of falling asleep were experimented with, and the results were catalogued in his usual meticulous way.

The Man fell asleep in deep concentration on a certain object. It could be anything: one of his apples, the little woman, the balloon, a traveler he had met on that particular day, a bird that flew by, and so on. And he revolved the image in his head, inspecting it from every angle and depth—its texture, its color, its smell. Perhaps the emotion it evoked.

Sometimes the object of his choosing would forge its image into the light of his dream, but in these cases he still had no control over their use or direction. They were loose pieces of a predetermined puzzle, though where they would fit was not to his discretion. Even their presence may have been coincidental. These facts were far from discouraging to The Man. The work itself was elating, and there were still other techniques to test.

He tried falling asleep without thinking of anything. 'Not empty, but open,' he would think. He stared into the distance behind his closed eyelids, past where the shadows contained weight. A dark space where gravity prevailed and pulled him from the inside, further inside until his own spirit had a mass, a true density. His spirit-body had the ability to move, to think, to half-speak. Environments materialized in the dark and he moved through them with an insatiable delight and fascination. He was not creating the things before him, but he was free to do with them as he wished. It was like an alternative life. Sometimes it was merely a revisitation to a previous situation in his other life, his 'real' life—the one on the orchard and before—which he could now change the outcome to. Sometimes it was a surrealist's scheme, Dadaist, with arbitrary habitats like the basement of a Greek restaurant(where he drank wine with sailors and his teeth went crooked), or neighborhoods in fictional cities, boardwalks, grottos, alleyways turned upside down, the front porch of an old house(where he levitated), or even the top of a moving city bus in the rain(where he stripped naked and attempted to smoke a wet cigarette).

There were other absurd environments, too, where he did absurd things that seemed, and were, suitable under their own circumstances. The Man could tolerate the random quirks which this technique yielded, and occasionally welcomed them, but what perturbed him was the ephemeral nature of his encounters, the lack of continuity. The people in his dreams were always meeting him for the first time, even if they had shared tea with him the sleep before. It was a lonely flaw, which The Man believed he could fix given enough serious practice, and there was plenty of time for that.

Outside of these more reserved methods of approaching sleep, The Man also exercised what he called, 'Loose Brain.' Loose Brain was another way of seeing after the eyes were closed. It consisted of a shallow focus, starting at the periphery where glowing dots and cords emerge, moving through the central area of vision while somehow evading direct examination. Over the surface of the eye the spectral dots and glowing cords coalesce, shimmy, squirm, and shake at low speeds, attempting to avoid being spotted. The faint and partial movement of their perpetual escape leaves an imprint on the eye, which is then registered in the brain according to the resemblance of the important. A line here is enough to look like the bend of a knee, which then makes a man in motion. A line there is enough to look like the bridge of a nose, which then becomes a face. First finding the glistening dust particles, then in charting a fraction of their trail and comparing its distinguishable points to the defining characteristics of a great database. The matches are innumerable, thus making the final act of pairing, or connecting the dots, an unconscious one.

Frequently, The Man experienced nightmares from Loose Brain. The line that looked like the bridge of a nose that then became the face usually became the face of the devil. The line that looked like the bend of a knee that then made a man in motion usually put The Man in motion and he was running for his life from the face of the devil.

It was impossible to be unaware of the perils of Loose Brain. It was the place where latent demons came out, right there in the thin film between eye and lid. But all manipulation of the mind comes with a certain amount of danger, and The Man was willing to endure those risks if they led to a greater understanding.

* * *

THE ORCHARD NEVER SUFFERED because of this dream business. The Man did not neglect a single duty, not one apple ever went to rot, and not one thirsty traveler ever went without water.

Some say that the orchard even thrived under the dream influence; that the apples had never grown so large, red, and sweet as they did then; that the well water had never been so clean and so cold. The Man himself was said to have been more brilliant and jovial than ever before. Volumes of poetry were written and sent off.

People along the trade route were baffled by the growing number of poems they found littering the roadside. Some asked The Man if he knew anything about these poems or their author. He told them that he knew a lot about both, but could not be sure what any of it meant. And then he always laughed.

One such questioner came just after the designated napping period one afternoon as The Man was outside his house standing in front of the mirror preparing his shaving things. His beard had grown splendidly during the recent, prolonged fever of his studies.

I can only guess what he looked like then, but I'm fairly sure this is a *good guess*:

But, then, the fever had subsided. The Man's endless experiments with sleep techniques and dreams had been distilled like a fine apple wine. They were refined so intricately in fact that there was no question to put to either of The Man's lives other than, 'What difference?'

The Man remembered the question from somewhere, a few places actually, and decided there was not a good enough answer to keep people from continuing to ask. Nonetheless, he felt very at peace and had nothing to show of this considerable achievement other than his beard and that seemed to be saying too much, or at least not what he wanted to be saying. The beard made his eyes look wild, like those of a person who has seen the oceans' depths or taken too many hallucinogens.

As The Man was about to begin shaving his beard, just as he dipped his razor into the warm water in the sink, the curious visitor arrived.

"Excuse me, sir," said the small voice of an old man, though it was muffled as if coming from under water. "Excuse me, sir, but we were hoping you might have some water for us."

The Man had been watching The Old Gentleman's slightly sunburned reflection in the mirror and had failed to see his lips moving, although the request had been made and heard clearly enough. He turned around slowly before answering, and as he did so he noticed The Old Gentleman was holding a fishbowl in his arms that was running low on water. In the bowl was a beautiful, bright gold fish too striking to be called a goldfish.

"Well," said The Man, "I don't know how I didn't see you coming up the road—my head must've been off somewhere else—but I'll get on that right away. You both look like you could use some water."

Not surprisingly, it was The Mute Gentleman's Fish who replied: "Yes, you are right, sir. We are both very much in need of some water. Thank you."

The Man smiled and escorted The Gentleman and his Polite Fish inside. He retrieved an ice cold glass of water for The Gentleman and a special bottle of tepid, distilled water from the cupboard to refill the fishbowl. It was not the first time a fish had passed through the orchard, so he was not unprepared for such a visitor.

Both of the new guests looked happy with their refreshments: The Gentleman gave a pleasant bow; The Fish swam in three excited circles then thanked The Man again and came to a sudden stop. The Fish seemed to *just think of something.*

"Sir," said The Fish, "I don't mean to impose on what appears to be your valued privacy, but you seem like a man that would be aware of happenings in these parts, and I'd like to ask you a question about something we found on the road."

"If I can answer your question then I will do so as honestly and thoroughly as possible." The Man anticipated what their finding was, as many others had discovered similar things, and he knew what the involved questions were, yet he decided that this time, for whatever reason, his response would stand true. He would answer as honestly and thoroughly as possible, provided The Fish said what The Man thought he would say next.

The Old Man and The Polite Fish
(just thinking of something)

And The Fish said exactly that: "Well, we were walking along the road yesterday as we have been for the past three days towards The Great River, which we think is another two days from here, where my master has decided to set me free because he is nearing the end of his life and doesn't want me to be alone after he dies.

"My master, who as you have noticed cannot speak, is very fond of beautiful colors and sounds and will interact with them however he can. You see, he is always tapping out rhythms on things and touching them as well as picking flowers and collecting other such ornamental things. And so he saw a red splotch on the side of the road that looked like the shredded paper of an exploded firecracker and was of course interested. But when we got closer to it we saw that it was a piece of red latex that seemed to be from a burst balloon. When he picked it up he discovered something beneath it that was even more amusing, and certainly more confusing than the balloon: it was a small piece of paper that had been folded several times over. So he unfolded the paper and we found there was a poem written on it—or at least part of a poem. He is still carrying it in his pocket now, but I remember what it said without having to look at it. It said:

Dunk your head
In the liquid forms
Of all these things
And your life will continue
In all directions of that shape.

"Now you can understand why these lines shook us. It was as if they were written specifically for our situation. And although that much is clear, my master and I disagree on the poem's meaning. He thinks that the poem is a statement about life after death and how the soul will carry on in everything, and now I'm pretty sure he intends to drown himself when we get to the river!"

Both Man and Master listened to The Fish intently. At the mention of the apparently planned suicide, The Man looked to The Old Gentleman who was close enough to death as it was. The Gentleman did not return the look, but kept fingering the bit of red latex that he had extracted from his pocket during the story.

The Fish continued: "And what I think, sir, is that the poem is more of a statement about life within life and how submitting yourself to the natural good forces of the world will open countless opportunities to you, thus expanding your experience. But we cannot be sure which one of us is right, sir, though we both believe our own explanations to be logical and true. So, you must tell us, do you know what this poem means? Or do you know who The Author of this poem is so that we might find that person and ask them what it means?"

The Fish ended his question by swimming another circle around his freshly replenished bowl then coming to a stop to await the answer. The Old Gentleman shoved the balloon shard back into his pocket and looked to The Man as well. The Man was touched by The Fish's words and was preparing to respond by fidgeting with the lemon-colored bouncy ball in his trouser pocket. He took the ball out, bounced it from floor to hand three times, returned it to his pocket, then began.

"Let me first say that your circumstance is not unusual, but extremely delicate seeing as it deals with the parting of a great bond. I am sorry to hear it. As for the poem and its meaning, perhaps you are both right. It is my belief that in analyzing things such as this the reader's personal interpretation takes on more importance than the author's intended meaning—as it should. What is poignant about being spoken to isn't necessarily the words being used, but the mere fact that they are being addressed to you. Though I will say that I seriously doubt the author in question would ever condone harming one's self, even for the supposed higher purpose of spiritual gain. And I am able to speak with some authority on the latter subject." The Man paused here for a respectful laugh, then cleared his throat to finish his short discourse. "I do know the author of the poem, very well. and his story is one that might take a moment to explain. If you are interested in hearing it then I will tell it to you, but I suggest we move into the lawn and have a glass of strong cider."

Master and Fish, both eager to hear more, were happy to accept a tall glass of strong cider and take comfortable positions in the lawn. The Man took his own glass onto the lawn after them and seated himself in the grass as well.

After a moment, he began to speak: "Each day there is a man on this orchard that writes a poem and sends it into the sky in a red balloon with the hope that the heavens will receive it and do as they please with his words. Once the poem disappears into the blue, The Man is gone too. Excuse the accidental rhyme there. But, carrying on, the next day, or sometimes later on in the same day even, a new man appears and, likewise, a new poem is written and sent off.

"Every day it is the same thing, but it is a different man. If you saw these men from one day to the next you might be inclined to say that it is but one man who writes these poems and sends them off. You might even be inclined to say that that man is me. And, although I do, in fact, have a memory of writing the poem that you are now holding in your pocket, I tell you that I am not that man anymore. I am changed. If I speak from memory, I can tell you that the very poem you hold is about the subject I am presently discussing. As for speaking in the moment, which is all that concerns me, I can say nothing about that poem because it no longer exists for me. It means nothing. It is a difficult thing I am trying to explain, but you seem to have some idea of where I'm going with all of this—yes?"

"Well, I think we understand a little of what you are saying," replied The Fish, speaking for both himself and his master. "But, if this is true, then maybe you could tell us about who you are now so that we might learn more about who you were when you composed this poem. After all, it was not long ago that we found it and we have not changed one bit since then—the poem still pertains to us!"

"Surely, I can do that! I didn't mean to seem inconsiderate, I am only trying to help in what little way that I can. First, before we continue, I believe more cider is in order. Good Sir? Good Fish?" The guests again accepted this generous offer and The Man went inside to tend to their empty glasses. When he returned they were full. "Now, where were we?"

"You were about to tell us about yourself," said The Fish promptly. "There's plenty of light and heat left in the day and we are in no hurry to spend it walking, so please don't leave anything out on our account. We definitely have the time. Besides, our direction seems to be confused since finding the poem, and I believe listening to you could straighten things out."

Enjoying the ridiculous fashion of this banter, The Man resituated himself in the spot he had been sitting before and prepared to keep it going. "I hope you are right there about straightening things out, but there shouldn't be an issue with the light, my friends, because the story I intend to tell is a short one. However, you are more than welcome to wait here until dusk before resuming your journey, or even stay overnight if you wish."

The Old Gentleman and The Fish appreciated the warm offer, but urged The Man to begin. With that he did: "I am a simple man and the years have treated me kindly. Exactly how many years that is I cannot say. I do not have that number in my head. As I said, I am a simple man, content. I try to avoid cluttering my brain with things that don't concern me—such as dates, money, superfluous names for people and things I can recognize by sight. Even my own name seems a sort of mystery to me. I rarely sign it. It would be like someone asking me to draw a portrait of myself then handing them a drawing of an infant. Surely, the picture would be of me, but of me as a child. And that is how my name appears to me— outdated, old. Likewise, I have memories that seem to belong to those other people, of which you need only hear about one. And even this one is not so much of a past experience as it is a feeling.

"It deals with my arrival here on the orchard. I will not say when, or how—remember that I am unable—but I will say that I had lost something, that I still don't know what that something was, and that I was tremendously sad over the loss. As you can see, I am not sad now. I have not been sad for quite some time. But do I still suffer from some ambiguous loss? No more than you or any other living creature does. It is in our nature. Just as it is in our nature to adapt. You ask me to tell you who I am now, but with each passing statement the previous statement becomes less true. Each moment is an adaptation, a transformation. Our experience is ever changing, and growing. And we must act in accordance. It is better for your present behavior to contradict your old beliefs than for your present beliefs to be contradicted by behaving out of old habit. Really, gentlemen, I am not sure how we got to this point, but is any of this of use to you?"

The Man's guests were startled by this short speech, even The Fish, who was used to swimming in circles. "I am having some difficulty making heads and tails of it," remarked The Fish, "but the way you said everything certainly was engaging. And now that I have had a moment to reflect, I think I am starting to make sense of it. But, kind sir, our situation is still very much at odds. What do you suggest we do?"

The Man scratched his cheek as he considered the question and remembered his large and pleasingly soft beard. He laughed. "I need to shave," he said, "but I will first give you my advice. Only, you must promise to not follow this advice if at any given time you don't want to." The guests vowed that they would not follow his advice, if they didn't want to that is. "Good," The Man continued, "then you should go to the river as you originally planned. And when you get there, do not do anything. Just sit and look into the river. Watch the steady movement of the water until you are moved as well to some sort of decision within yourselves. Then you will know what to do."

The Master and Fish took this advice silently and proudly. They felt as though The Man were putting his confidence in them, and by doing so they put their confidence in themselves. It was an invigorating confidence they now had and they wished to start their journey again immediately. Dusk was approaching soon enough, and the walk would be a pleasant one at night.

The Master got up from his seat in the grass and took the fishbowl in his arms. They thanked The Man in their own respective ways: The Fish with several "thank yous" and excited circles; The Master with a polite bow and wide grin. The Man thanked them in return, then watched as they took off up the hill, got back on the road, and disappeared.

It had been a very nice afternoon talking with The Fish and Master so that The Man was still smiling when he got back to his shaving things at the sink. The smile had not yet broken by the time he was nearly finished— only the upper lip to go. The Man laughed at his reflection in the mirror and the absurd hair of his mustache. He thought it was a very funny thing and that it made him much more approachable than that big, bushy beard he had just gotten rid of. He decided it might not be a bad thing to keep for awhile—so he did.

* * *

RESUMING THE LAST RECORDS of The Man's life, right where we left him last. The balloon containing the laugh-marked stationery is long lost in the now fully bright blue sky. It is the hottest part of the day on the orchard. Which is not to say it is hot at all—it is actually very temperate—but it is the part of the day designated for dreaming. If the orchard were situated on a different trade route, somewhere further down or over, you might call it 'siesta' like those other people who are also very well acquainted with dreaming. But here it is not called anything.

Though it does not have a title, The Man knows by habit or instinct what this time of day represents. Accordingly, his vest and boots are removed. His pillow is fluffed.

As the mattress awaits the warm, lean body of its resident dreamer, The Man sits nearby at his writing desk in bestockinged feet. The pen rests in his hand over a blank sheet of stationery and his head is clear.

The strange feeling of anticipation that The Man has experienced all morning seems to manifest itself in his fingertips. They are buzzing with things that he cannot bring himself to write because there are no words for them. There is a whole world coursing through his blood and firing off at random throughout his nervous system. It is a convergence of memory, creation, sight, and sound. A speculation about things known and unknown. It is the very stuff of his collective dreams and lives coming together at once, consciously merging their forms from the static.

Although there is joy, there is no longer the ability to laugh. Or, for that matter, there is no longer the ability to do anything with the body. The Man's hand is arrested in its hovering position, absorbed by a curious sensation not unlike finding something that was never truly lost. The pen, left dangling in the unmoving hand, makes contact with the otherwise unblemished stationery. A tiny black dot is created, a speck of ink, a little period, a distant balloon on an indefinite horizon.

The fierce light of the day shooting through the house reflects off the stationery. The glare spreads outwards from the tiny black dot, covering the page and enveloping the surface of the desk in whole. The shining white of the vast light source leaks over the floorboards, creeping over the sheets of the awaiting bed, climbing over the trunk and icebox, the helium tank, the balloons, and, finally, swallowing The Man himself, suspended in his chair over the last record of his known existence: a tiny black dot on an expanding white page, an inconsequential speck of ink, a little period like a distant balloon on an infinite horizon.

AFTER LIFE

I WAS WALKING, SOMEWHERE, ON A ROAD that winds through the great countryside between Paris and Sad Francisco. The weather was fine—blue sky bluer than usual, a soft breeze keeping my sweat at bay—but my mood was dissolute. I was a bit downcast for no reason at all. There was nowhere I needed to be, yet I continued to walk because of the strange temperament I found myself in, asking myself, 'What is it I am searching for? Why this feeling?'

These questions repeated themselves over and over in my head. They repeated themselves so many times that I did not think about them anymore. I simply kept on walking and taking in the countryside. Despite how wonderful the scenery was, and the endorphins that must have been running through my body from the prolonged exertion, I still felt a little funny, a little sad. I tried not to think about that either. In effect, I thought about nothing and my journey became automatic, uninhibited. My feet carried me on the most natural course and I made no attempt to intervene.

It is impossible to say how much time or distance passed before I came out of it, but I saw something just ahead of me in the road that caught my attention. It appeared to be a bloody rag and the notion of blood alerted my senses. However, when I came upon it I saw that I was quite mistaken. It was just a burst balloon, probably popped to some child's dismay by a piece of windblown debris, or just plain carelessness on the part of the child, and then left there on the ground to be forgotten about. This practical explanation put me back at ease and I picked up the sad balloon only to find my senses alerted in a different way. Tangled in the latex was a tiny piece of paper, which I found not to be so tiny after all when I reversed its six, meticulous folds. What truly made it curious was that there was nothing on either side of this paper. It seemed odd for someone to take such efforts in folding a piece of paper in that manner when it had nothing on it. The thing really intrigued me, I don't know why. Neither do I know why I picked up the balloon and paper both and stuck them into my pockets as I then resumed walking.

I did not push these things out of my thoughts as I had so easily done with the previous subject. Several times I even took the paper into my hands, observed it, and asked, 'Where did it come from? What does it mean? And why?'

The repetition of these questions put me into a different trance than the one before, more deliberate. For a moment, I contemplated the nature of the questions themselves and my mood lightened at the broad spectrum to which they might be suited. 'For the time being,' I thought, 'I will keep things as simple as possible: the balloon and the paper; red and white,' and so on. The terms in which I thought that day were very funny, but, as I said, the mood itself was a funny one and none of it can quite be explained.

Though it is an unnecessary detail to add, I would guess that this behavior lasted for three days—meaning the taking out of the piece of paper, the inspection of it, the asking of those questions. I can only recall sleeping twice, briefly. Both times my sleep was interrupted by a dream that I can't remember, but for some reason makes me think of things associated with carnivals: laughter, of course, and that feeling in your stomach that you get while riding certain rickety rides, like you might come unhinged and go floating into the sky. They weren't disturbing dreams, but they were certainly out of the ordinary and made sleep very difficult.

By the third day I was exhausted. I knew that I could go on no longer without a good meal, some good rest, and a lot of water. Not to say I knew exactly where I was going anyway, but I knew that it couldn't be that far—I wouldn't be able to make it. Luckily, some short distance ahead of me I spotted an orchard of sorts whose trees crosshatched a steep hill with the same precision in which my piece of paper had been folded(a detail I did not notice at the time). There were no other options for me then. I had to stop immediately, so I stopped there.

* * *

THE HOUSE WAS A SMALL ONE positioned at the bottom of the orchard, so I had to manage the hill in my weary state to get to it. The easiest way of doing this was to propel myself downward using gravity as my source of propulsion. I leaned forward and let my body be taken by the force and I barely had the energy to keep my body upright as I ran at full speed, almost gliding over the spongy green surface of the hill. I avoided hitting any trees, but I did notice that they were growing brilliant red apples on them, being that they stood out considerably against the overwhelming green hue of the area and the bright white, flat blossoms on the trees.

Reaching the bottom, I had expelled the last of my energy in keeping myself from toppling over and needed to rest for a moment. I laid down in the grass right in front of the house and put my hands behind my head as I caught my breath.

An apple fell from one of the trees further up the hill from me, landing safely in the grass and immediately gaining momentum in its descent. When it smacked me in the ribs I awoke. It was a gorgeous apple I had been struck with, and I wasted no time in devouring it. Then I saw not far from me was a trench with a large net at its backside, and in the trench lay several delicious looking apples. Quickly, I gathered as many as I could in my shirt and hat and went back to have a seat on the front porch of the house to eat.

I had already eaten three or four apples before realizing that the door to the house was propped open by a large helium tank. I called inside to see if anyone was home, but received no answer. There were a pair of boots just inside the door and I could see a mattress, and a desk too, with a piece of paper laying on its surface as if someone had recently been sitting there. By all appearances of the house, at least what I could see of it from the doorway—which turned out to be the entirety of the house, excluding the contents of the cupboards and drawers—I concluded that the owner had just stepped out for a bit and would be back pretty soon. As for the boots, perhaps this man(I knew it was a man by the size and look of the boots) sought to enjoy a little barefoot walkabout—the grass would surely feel nice on the feet.

In any case, it was nearing dusk on the orchard and the sky seemed to gloss over with sparkling blue ice. A barefoot walkabout seemed reasonable enough when it was light out, but not in the dark when you might step on some sharp object and hurt yourself. With all things considered, I expected The Man to return any time now.

For an entire week I waited in that way for The Man to return home without infringing upon his right to privacy. Sure, I ate when I was hungry and drank when I was thirsty—there was plenty to go around—but I did not disrupt anything in the home unless out of necessity. For the most part I stuck to the porch, and even started earning my keep by doing what chores needed to be done, though there were very few. The orchard basically took care of itself. All I had to do was collect the apples from the trench so they would not rot, and give water to travelers in need.

Concerning those travelers, I encountered a number of them throughout the week and took to asking them questions that pertained to the missing owner of the orchard. Some did not know The Man, as they had never traveled that particular road before. Some seemed to have been well acquainted with him and shared my concern for his absence. They said it was not in his character to leave the orchard in such a way, and they also told me he would be grateful that I had assumed the responsibility under the circumstance. Then they remarked on the physical similarities between myself and The Man. These things, as comforting as they were to hear, only raised my suspicions regarding the whereabouts of The Man. What exactly was *the circumstance*?

I resolved to do a thorough search of his home and belongings in hopes of gaining some insight into his disappearance—some sort of clue as to what might have happened. I had already eyed the helium tank with some curiosity, as the balloon and paper had not ceased burning a hole in my pocket and brain—so the search started there. In the vicinity of the helium tank, which is to say in the vicinity of the house, being that it was so small, I immediately found a duffel bag full of uninflated red balloons just like the one I had been brooding over. It did not strike me as unusual, and I realized that all along I must have suspected the connection, thus my deep and genuine investment in the continuing mystery. I had to get to the very bottom of it all, no matter what it took.

The house may have been a small one, as already noted, but the information which was hidden within it began to paint an infinitely larger and more wonderful picture. Each step turned up more details. In every drawer, nook, and corner, under every floorboard, there was page after page of autobiographical notes(to which all the previous accounts are owed.) The Man's handwriting was extremely legible and his attention to detail very elucidating. All of my efforts then went into reading.

I have already said that I ate when I was hungry and drank when I was thirsty. Sleeping, however, was a different story. When I grew tired I would lie down on the bed and shut my eyes only to wake feeling as if I had never slept at all. The passages I had read invaded my sleeping head, repeating themselves in tangible dimensions formatted in the dreams. It was as if I were watching firsthand what The Man had seen, in full color, and it was always accompanied by the same strange feeling I experienced while sleeping on the road just before arriving at the orchard—like my stomach was first floating up, then down, then I would suddenly awake.

It took weeks to get through everything. Reading the papers, organizing them, cataloging. By the end of it I was completely worn out, body and mind, but my efforts had yielded a fantastic result: the warm feeling of being just fine. Everything was explained explicitly in The Man's writing, save for the one piece of paper that had been left on his writing desk with nothing but a single touch of the pen tip, and his present whereabouts, but I was satisfied with the implied answers that his records pointed to.

With everything pieced together and played out in front of me by way of dream, I did not lament the loss of The Man, although I felt as if I knew him personally(and even seem to have taken to communicating in a voice like his own—as if it weren't enough to look like him!) and it was clear that he would not be coming back. Instead, I smiled and felt just fine. That is not to say my own abstract search was over, or that I did not still have some sadness in me, it just meant that this particular stage would soon be over. There was only one last thing I felt needed to be done in his name, and I held myself responsible for carrying it out.

* * *

THE MEMORIAL SERVICE WAS TO BE HELD at the bottom of the orchard, directly in front of the house, where The Man once stood in the flesh on many occasions to sing his plights and praises to the heavens. I sent out several invitations in shiny red balloons and requested that the recipients come the following Sunday, bringing with them anyone who might wish to honor The Man. The turnout was better than I expected. It was absolutely astonishing.

Beginning at sunrise, large groups of people started showing up at the orchard. To each of them I gave a red balloon until finally there were no more balloons to give and the helium tank was empty. The entire orchard was filled with people who had known The Man and people who had only heard of him. They were all dressed in black.

Despite the popular attire, it was not an overall somber affair. Some did quietly mourn, but some celebrated. Closure was provided to those in need, and to others a word of possible explanation arose. Amidst the exchange of fond memories, everyone discussed what they believed may or may not have transpired in the time that led up to The Man's disappearance. Ultimately, some said that a woman was involved. That The Man fell in love with her and they ran off together. Some suggested foul play. Some said that he simply went mad.

It is my own opinion that these theories, which are all they amount to, are false. After pouring over The Man's every last personal record and reliving them in dreams had in the bed he once slept in, after doing the chores he once performed, after living on the sweet, sparse diet of various apple treats and little more, after essentially almost becoming him, I believe that there was a greater force at work—something incomprehensible, divine. By all the miracles in the world, I believe that The Man finally caught up to the dreams he had for so long chased, and somehow sewed his body up into the gas-fabric of his soul, where it is both preserved and un-needed, and contradiction meets in a white spot of ulti-mate, deliberate joy. And in order to truly pay our re-spects to The Man, I believe all we can do is follow suit by chasing after our own curious visions, seeking them within ourselves with patience, kindness, and compas-sion in our hearts.

If there are any arguments as to the validity of my own theory, they are welcomed. I have provided this se-lection of The Man's notes to encourage you to not forget Him, and to reevaluate the specific events shown from his life so that you *can* draw your own conclusions. There is no harm to be done in questioning, in searching, so long as we are able to return with peace like that which we found on the orchard on the evening of The Man's memorial service.

I remember it well, with a peculiar, joyful sadness. It was an illuminated dusk, mimicking the near afterglow of the memorial service itself, and a wave of silence fi-nally passed through the tired congregation as soft and sincere as a head bowing slightly in prayer. Speculation ceased from the mouths of gossipers and there was a mo-ment where it didn't matter anyway. In the wild bluebon-net colored sky, flying in zig-zag patterns and alternating letters of the alphabet, there were a few flocks of cloud white birds whose formations succeeded in spelling nothing before they moved on, continuing with their separate journeys and destinies.

Below where the birds had just left, standing amongst the crowd in the middle of the yard, I felt it was time to release the balloon I had been holding all day in honor of The Man's memory and I watched as it began to rise. All at once, fingers and thumbs parted across the orchard, strings slipped upward through the narrow gaps the parting fingers created, and the rest of the balloons trailed after my own. And together they made their casual ascent, slowly escaping into the cool blue opening of the sky beyond where, surely, something better exists.

ENJOY: AN ILLUSTRATED FABLE

ENJOY: AN ILLUSTRATED FABLE

ENJOY: AN ILLUSTRATED FABLE

ENJOY: AN ILLUSTRATED FABLE

ENJOY: AN ILLUSTRATED FABLE

ENJOY: AN ILLUSTRATED FABLE

Font is an award winning writer and filmmaker and the author of I AM NO ONE: A Collection that New York Times Best Selling Author and #GIRLBOSS Sophia Amoruso called "Gorgeous and massive!" His screenplay credits include SEX/ABSURD, THE SYMPATHIST, and Orion Pictures' DREAMLAND, which the New York Times called "a smart, understated sex comedy." His first feature as a writer/director was A Holiday Comedy About Suicide called MADNESS, FAREWELL, which premiered at the Napa Valley Film Festival and is currently streaming on Amazon and other platforms.